wild lies and secret truth

wild lies and secret truth

Matt Tullos

BROADMAN
& HOLMAN
PUBLISHERS

Nashville, Tennessee

0-8054-1765-6

Published by Broadman & Holman Publishers, Nashville, Tennessee
Page Design: Anderson Thomas Design, Nashville, Tennessee
Typesetter: PerfecType, Nashville, Tennessee
Editorial Team: Vicki Crumpton, Janis Whipple, Kim Overcash

Dewey Decimal Classification: F
Subject Heading: HIGH SCHOOLS—FICTION
Library of Congress Card Catalog Number: 98-40555

Library of Congress Cataloging-in-Publication Data

Tullos, Matt, 1963–
    Wild Lies and Secret Truth / Matt Tullos.
        p.   cm. — (Summit High series ; bk 3.)
    Summary: Clipper and Jenny find themselves in an unexpected whirlwind
romance, while Autumn pursues her project of helping the school custodian Felix
get his high school degree.
    ISBN 0-8054-1765-6 (pbk.)
    [1. High schools—Fiction. 2. Schools—Fiction. 3. Christian life—Fiction.]
I. Title. II. Series: Tullos, Matt, 1963–   Summit High series ; 3.
PZ7.T82316Wi 1999
[Fic]—dc21

                                                                    98-40555
                                                                        CIP
                                                                         AC

1 2 3 4 5 02 01 00 99 98

Dedication

To Isaac

Special thanks to Janis, Robin, Bucky,
Kim, and Lissa

The lunch bell sent students at Summit High rushing through the halls. Someone jumped on Justin's back. The initial shock changed to a knowing smile as Justin realized that no one but his friend Clipper would do that to him.

"Tonight is *the* night," Clipper said loudly, over the clamor of the student body. "The big date."

"She hasn't canceled?"

"Not yet," Clipper said smiling.

"I think it's going to happen," Justin said, sounding slightly amazed.

"No doubt, man."

"Are you ready?"

"Justin, I've been ready all year," Clipper replied. "I mean, if you had told me in December that I'd have a date with Jenny Elton, I'd have laughed in your face." He shook his head. "I take that back. I would have slugged you for joking about it. But tonight, it's gonna happen."

"So what's the plan?" Justin asked, weaving through the crowd of students.

"I called her last night and asked her to describe a perfect date, and after we got past the Hawaii and Leonardo DeCaprio deal she mentioned art museums and seafood."

Justin smiled, a bit surprised by Clipper's straightforward approach, "That's very cool. You just asked her?"

"Exactly."

"And she told you."

"Right."

"Are you going to do what she considers to be the perfect date?"

"Close to perfect. DeCaprio would be way too much competition," Clipper replied.

Justin shook his head, amazed that his shy friend was acting with such confidence. "I don't know what book you've been reading. I'm gonna have to give that a try sometime."

Clipper slapped Justin on the back hard and goofily said, "Yeah. Right. As if you don't know the stuff Kandi likes. You two are practically married."

"What?!"

"Well, you are," Clipper laughed.

"Are not."

"I mean, take away all the sexual stuff. I know. I know. You two are keeping up with the whole purity deal. But it's spooky the way you think alike. I mean, you guys are in some kind of oneness zone. I thought *I* knew you well. I've known you since you lost your cookies all over the cafeteria floor in third grade when I explained how they made the mystery meat, but *you and Kandi* . . . You've only known each other for a couple of months, and now you're on the same mental wavelength. You're like an old married couple."

"Oh shut up! You're making me sick. Can we just change the subject? We're so far from marriage."

"OK," Clipper said brightly. Then his face clouded over. "So . . ." he began, obviously having lost his train of thought.

"So, I think you were telling me about Jenny and your wooing plans."

"Wooing plans?" Clipper made a face.

They paused momentarily as they hopped into Justin's car. They pulled into the long line of cars full of students enjoying the privilege of avoiding the lunchroom at Summit and heading to "hamburger row."

"So . . . feeling pretty good about the whole thing?" Justin continued.

"I guess. After she backed out two times I was—"

"Clipper! Legitimate excuses. She didn't have any choice either time. I'm sure if Jenny wasn't interested, she'd use one of the 'organizing the sock drawer' cop-out lines. She wants to be there, otherwise she would have backed out totally."

"But—"

"Totally," Justin interrupted with an I'm-up-to-my-earlobes-with-this tone. "Stop worrying about it! You said it yourself. You've wanted to spend some time with the girl. Tonight's your chance. Have a great time, but gargle before you leave the house."

"My breath?" Clipper asked, cupping his hand over his mouth and nose for a quick halitosis check.

"Oh, yeah . . ." Justin said with pseudo-seriousness. Then he changed his tone. "Are you nervous?"

"Yep. I'm nervous all right," Clipper said.

"Just relax and once you get going, everything will settle down. Just take it slow."

Clipper looked at Justin, narrowing his eyes defensively, "What do you mean take it slow?"

"Clipper, what I mean is . . . I just don't want you to build this thing up so big that when it goes down in flames—"

"When? Did you say *when?*" Clipper couldn't believe that Justin was already predicting an end to the relationship before it even started.

"Oops, I mean *if—if* things fizzle out you won't be so freaked."

Silence.

Then Clipper spoke up, "This is our first date. I'm not going to shove my class ring on her thumb or anything."

"I know. I know. But you've got to admit, you're treating this like it was the beginning of a lifetime relationship. I just don't want you to be bummed out if she turns out not to be into the date as much as you are."

"Let's drop the subject," Clipper said as he looked out the window.

Another long uncomfortable pause. Clipper's head pounded. *Why is Justin being so negative?* he wondered.

⊂‑⊐

After lunch, Melissa began her endless barrage of questions for Ms. Swinson, her algebra teacher. It was like her right arm was connected to a spring. Every time Ms. Swinson answered a question, Melissa's arm popped back up to ask another one.

"So, like, are we gonna have any multiple choice questions?" Melissa asked.

"Uh, Melissa, don't expect any surprises," Ms. Swinson said dryly.

Pop! Melissa's arm jumped back up.

"So, like, are we gonna have to know what we covered at the, like, beginning of the year?" Melissa, a cute, dark-haired, slightly overweight junior prided herself on asking more questions than any junior in Summit High's fifty-six-year history. Her mouth was in a state of perpetual movement due to her powerful addiction to chewing gum and gossip. She also gloried in using the word *like* constantly. In fact, it was doubtful she'd even be able to speak at all if the word were banned from her vocabulary.

"Let's just go over this thing again, Melissa. There will be a test. Like . . . Monday afternoon. Are you . . . like . . . getting this so far, Melissa?"

"Like . . . yes," Melissa replied coyly.

"Good," Ms. Swinson continued. "It will be an Algebra II exam." Swinson, a fifty-ish teaching veteran of twenty years, spoke slowly and deliberately as if she were speaking to a Ugandan who spoke very little English. Melissa smiled, and several students giggled.

Melissa decided she had finally gotten under the veteran teacher's thick exterior.

"It will not be discussion. It will not be true-false. It will not be story problems." Ms. Swinson sounded the words out in super-slow speed. "Aaaaallllgeeeebraaaa. Algebra. We will have formulas and numbers and lots of variables. You do remember variables don't you, Melissa?"

She's losing it. Isn't she? Melissa thought. *I've been working on this all year and on the third to last day of my junior year, I think I finally did it.* She looked at her classmates who smiled. She'd been playing this chess game of sanity all year, hoping, in a sick way, for Ms. Swinson to jump on her desk and scream at the top of her lungs. "Melissa! You thankless, brainless queen of the dumb questions! I want you out of this door. I want you out of my life! Ahhhh!" Melissa pouted. It wouldn't be today after all. Ms. Swinson seemed tense but in control.

Swinson continued, "Melissa, I suggest you save us both the hassle and study for this test. Agreed?"

Melissa plastered a fake smile on her face that vanished as quickly as it came.

Carla, an attractive junior with long, wavy brown hair, sat next to Melissa. She shook her head as she blew her hair out of her eyes. Carla and Melissa were friends, even though they ran with different groups at Summit. Carla, a popular girl with social status, simply endured Melissa's embarrassing dialogues with teachers and guys to catch the latest gossip. Melissa also amused Carla with her ability to catch people off guard by saying things others might think but never say aloud. Melissa needed Carla's ties to gather more gossip.

"Do you have any other insights or questions, Melissa?" Ms. Swinson asked.

"Nope, uh, maybe one."

"OK, what is it?"

"If I, like, flunk the class. Are you gonna, like, get to teach me again?"

Swinson smiled and said, "Not if I have anything to do with it."

"So are you and Tim over—as in never seeing each other again?" Carla asked Jenny in the parking lot after school.

"We were over weeks ago," Jenny said. She looked away from Carla, scanning the exiting cars.

"That's not the way Tim put it."

"Believe what you want to. I am not tied to him." Jenny clenched her teeth.

"Why not?" Carla asked.

"Because," Jenny said, then paused, choosing her words carefully. "It wasn't going to work."

"Like I believe that," Carla said suspiciously.

"Carla, he's in college now, and I want a life outside my room for the next two years. Isn't that enough of a reason?" Jenny hoped her look would silence Carla. It didn't work.

"I don't know. I think he'd be worth waiting around for," Carla said, smiling devilishly.

"I don't even want to get into this. If you like the guy so much maybe you should date him. I've got his phone number at Notre Dame if you're interested," Jenny said.

Carla quickly changed the subject. "So, what are you doing tonight?"

"I'm going out," Jenny said.

"You're kidding! You didn't even tell me. Who with?"

"Just somebody," Jenny said. "Can you believe it's this hot in May?"

"Whoa! Back up, weather girl," Carla said with a smile. "What somebody are you going out with?"

"It's just a . . . date. With a friend. Just a friend. Nobody you'd know," Jenny replied.

"At least tell me his name," Carla demanded.

"There's Mom. See ya!" Jenny said as she ran away.

"You try to be a friend and this is what you get," Carla yelled after her. "No, go ahead. Don't tell me! Fine!"

Felix, the quirky Cajun custodian at Summit High School, stuck his head into room 203. He could always count on seeing Autumn in the newly restored computer room, working late on papers and projects. And Autumn always turned her attention away from the computer to talk to him. Even though Autumn was half Felix's age, she was like an older sister to him. Felix knew he would miss her company this summer.

"Hey there, Ms. Autumn. Whatchu doin' there. Surfin' dat Internet?"

Autumn jumped slightly, "Oh, hey Felix. I was just working on a project proposal for my honors elective class."

"Dat's the one Ms. Hamilton teaches."

"Right. This summer I'm doing a project for college credit. It'll also give me enough credits to skip my sophomore year and be a junior at Summit this fall. And . . ." Autumn took a breath and felt a little nervous though she couldn't quite understand why. "And I was wondering if maybe you could help me with it."

"Autumn! You talkin' bout ole Felix helpin' you with a class project? Dat would be great! You need me to build a platform or clean off the tables after you finished? What it be? One of dem exploding volcano models?"

Autumn laughed. "No, Felix. No exploding volcano models. Nothing like that."

"Oh," Felix grunted, obviously a little disappointed. "Den whatchu need ole Felix for?"

"Felix, don't you remember how you said a few weeks ago that you wish you would have stayed in school and gotten your diploma?" Autumn reminded him as she turned away from the monitor and looked at him squarely, "I want to help you do it!"

"Dat's your project?"

"That's what I want it to be. I want you to help me do this, and I'll help you get your high school diploma!"

Autumn could see the walls around Felix go up. He sat down and crossed his arms. The friendly forty-year-old custodian evolved into a shy little boy as he looked away.

"So what's wrong?" she asked.

"I don't think dat would help you no ways."

"Why do you say that?"

"I was just *talkin'* the other day, just blabbin' on. Didn't mean nothin' by dat. I ain't smart. Ain't never been smart like you or anybody else 'round here. They gived me tests when I was 'bout ten and said I wouldn't amount to much of anything. Besides, I don't need no diploma. I like my job. Got lots of friends here."

"But you can do it, Felix." Autumn assured him.

"No, I can't," Felix said assertively.

"Why not?" Autumn asked. "It'll be fun."

Felix got up and shook his head. "You just goin' to have to find someone else for your summer project. You my good friend, but I can't do that. Jus' can't. No way. No how."

"Felix, just let me explain this whole thing to you—"

"No can do. I'll be a talkin' to you later."

Autumn sighed in frustration as she watched Felix walk out the door. *Oh well, there goes a 2000-word project proposal,* she thought to herself.

After Melissa got home, she dialed Jenny's number several times. Melissa adored the phone. Her parents had let her have a phone line with a wireless headset to cut down on chiropractic visits. Her neck became sore from contorting her head to hold the phone securely on her collarbone. She was destined for a telemarketing career. "Stupid answering machines. Like, why do people even buy them!" she vented to herself. "I'll try once more and then—fine, ignore me," she said as if talking to the keypad on the telephone.

Melissa dialed and Jenny answered, "Hello?"

"Where have you been, woman?" Melissa shouted while waving a finger in the air.

"Oh . . . hey Melissa. I just got in." Jenny said.

"Just got in? Just got in?? School was out two hours ago."

Jenny laughed, "You are such a control freak. I went shopping with my mom. She picked me up at school."

"Clothes?"

"Yes."

"For tonight?"

"Melissa!"

"Don't Melissa me, girl."

"How did you know about tonight?" Jenny asked, knowing she had been slightly secretive about her date with Clipper.

"Seriously, Jenny. I thought you knew me better than that. Everybody within five square miles of Summit could tell that Clipper has this, like totally overblown crush on you. I'm embarrassed for him. He's like a one-man fan club. I asked him about you and he said in a very hushed, but completely excited voice that you two had a love connection, a romantic tryst, a mono-a-mono, you'll be getting jiggy with the Clippster."

"He did not!" Jenny replied, eyes wide.

"OK, he didn't say that; but he did say that you're going out," Melissa said.

"All right, already. We're going out," Jenny surrendered. "What do you want me to do? Take an ad out in the newspaper? Why are you making such a big deal out of this whole thing?"

"Because you're like Julia Roberts and he's like . . . Lyle Lovett on a bad hair day."

Jenny shook her head in disgust and said, "Oh, get out! He's sweet. He's funny."

"Great personality, huh?" Melissa said as she tossed a few Skittles in her mouth. "That is the biggest laugh. Problem is, you have to be seen with him."

"Now you're making me mad."

"I'm just kidding, Jenny! Don't be so hypersensitive." Melissa took a few sips of her Diet Dr. Pepper as she sat on a futon in her bedroom and began her barrage of questions—"So what you wearing? Where you going? When's he coming?—"

"Look, why don't you wire me for the date and you'll know everything?"

"You mean I could tape the whole—"

"Melissa!" Jenny screamed. "Here's the deal, we're going to Jaques Seafood and the Christel DeHaan Fine Arts Center."

"Whoa! The Fine Arts Center? I'm impressed. That'll be a first for Clipper."

Jenny heaved a deep frustrated sigh. "Well, nice talking to you."

"So, what'd you get to wear? Something slinky?"

"No, it's not. You are so nosy. I'll talk to you later, Melissa."

"Don't you think its a little early to date? I mean, like, Tim's only been out of your life for about two months."

"Thanks for reminding me. Life goes on . . . I'm hanging up now."

"OK, Tell Lyle—I mean Clipper—I said—"

"BYE!" Jenny said as she hung up the phone.

Melissa took her head set off and said to herself, "Me? Nosy?"

When Kandi got home from school, she opened her E-mail. She retrieved a letter from Troy, a friend who faced a continuing battle with AIDS. It was addressed to her and almost ten other friends.

Hey guys. I just wanted to tell you that I'm going back to the hospital. I don't know what they'll be able to do for me except stabilize my blood count and buy me a little time. Don't know why some people live a long time with it and then others, like me, well, not so long. AIDS is a nasty thing. If there is any hint of a weakness in my body, the virus finds it and blows it up into a huge problem. The more I fight, the closer it seems to be. I used to hope for a cure, but now I think I'm just resigned to the fact that I'll be gone before a Nobel-prize-winning cure is found. I know there's life after all of this is over, but I don't want to leave all of you. Please continue to pray. Thanks for the visits and the prayers. I'm always reminded of what real love is about when you reach out to me. As before, you'll be able to reach me on the sixth floor of St. Luke's.

Kandi wiped her tears and laid down on her bed. She closed her eyes and prayed for answers to a ton of questions.

Clipper's parents assaulted him with a thousand and one questions about Jenny. They didn't know anything about her since she wasn't a member of Grove Community Church and wasn't active in school sports. He refused to tell them exactly where he was going.

"We're going to eat at a nice restaurant, and then we're going to see something," Clipper said.

"What restaurant?" Mr. Hayes asked inquisitively.

"We might have a coupon," his mom said quickly with her pointer finger in the air.

"Coupon?" Clipper said rolling his eyes, "Did you just say *coupon*? As if I'm actually going to use a coupon on a date."

"PG? PG13?"

"Mom it is not even a movie! It's like G! Totally G! Just trust me!"

"We'll trust you until midnight, then we'll ground you," Clipper's dad said in a Clint Eastwood voice.

Clipper took a final look into the rearview mirror. He frowned, smiled, winked and pointed at the mirror, nodded, and tried out every possible expression he might use on this date. He obsessed over his monumental lack of social graces. His new shirt and jeans, bought just for this night, weren't making up for his lack of good looks, either.

Clipper's eyes darted to the digital car clock and then to the pocket watch clipped to his belt loop. *Could I actually be sitting in the car in front of her house fifteen minutes ahead of time?* He shook his head, disgusted with himself. *Being way early for a date is the greatest sign of utter dweebness. I'll drive around a little.*

As he shifted into drive and slowly pulled away from her house, he thought about Kandi, who had told him she prayed he would not get too emotionally involved so early. He shook his head as he remembered Justin's warning that seemed almost a carbon copy statement of what Kandi had said. *They don't even think I should be here,* Clipper speculated.

After three times around the block his heart began to race. He performed a few breathing exercises he thought might settle him down. "This is crazy. She backed out on me twice before. I'm so blind! This is so token of her! She doesn't want to go out tonight." He almost left for the 7-11 down the road to call her and tell her he was sick. Or better yet just say, "Look, I know you don't want to go out with me. You could go out with anyone you wanted, so I'll spare you the inconvenience of—" He banged his hand on the steering wheel in anger. His car swerved into the oncoming lane and the car traveling opposite him leaned on the horn. Clipper swerved and regained his determination. "All right. I'm going. I've waited too long for this and I'm not backing out now."

Clipper drove back to the street that bordered Jenny's home. As soon as his car came to a stop the porch light switched on. As he stepped out of the car, his panic subsided. He realized he had nothing to lose. He would simply treat her as if she were a friend (which she was), and if she seemed standoffish (which she might), so be it.

Before he could ring the doorbell, Jenny's dad opened the door and smiled like Clipper was his long-lost nephew.

"Hi, Clipper. Haven't seen you since we met at the BurgeRama."

Mr. Elton's jovial mood took Clipper by surprise. "Oh, yeah BurgeRama . . ."

"Don't you remember?"

Clipper jumped in, "Right. Sure. I remember."

"You uh . . . kind of look different without your BurgeRama uniform."

"Thanks . . . I guess."

"Come on in. Jenny's really excited about tonight."

Clipper's mouth opened slightly as he failed to conceal his surprise.

Mr. Elton continued, "Yep, she hasn't stopped talking about it. I thought I saw you pull up a few minutes ago and then the car—"

"That was me. I noticed that I was really early and—"

"Hey, I like early, especially on the other end of a date. You know what I mean?" Mr. Elton said, laughing.

Clipper laughed out of sheer instinct. He went into a world of his own as he replayed the part about Jenny talking about tonight nonstop. *Did he actually say that?*

Mr. Elton gestured to the couch in the living room and Clipper sat down. He felt self-conscious about everything, even how he sat. *Cross the legs or not? Not. Hands in pockets? One. No, that's gotta look slouchy. Take the right hand out.*

"You've had a pretty exciting year. I went to a couple of games."

"Really?" Clipper blurted out in surprise.

"Sure did. I remember that one game where you made the last shot after you missed a free throw and won the game. That had to have been most exciting high school game I've seen in a long while."

Clipper's confidence grew. "Uh, thanks, I mean, yeah, that was a really, really exciting game."

"Hey, Clipper." Jenny said as she walked into the living room.

Clipper's heart jumped. Jenny stood there, looking gorgeous even without the heavy coats of makeup or jewelry or expensive clothes that other girls wore to impress guys. Not that she couldn't afford it. Her blonde hair and fair complexion didn't need much help. This was a moment to memorize for Clipper. *Glad I didn't back out,* he thought.

"So, what's the plan?" Mr. Elton asked.

"The plan is—" Clipper began.

"To go out to eat and then go to the impressionist show at the fine arts center," Jenny announced with a twinge of high society in her voice.

"Impressionists. Is that like Jim Carrey, Martin Short, Kevin Neylon?" Mr. Elton said laughing.

"You are such a nerd, Dad. It's like van Gogh, Sarat, Renoir, and Lautrec," Jenny said, and then whispered to Clipper, "He only acts that way when I have a date. Otherwise, he's a pretty cool dad."

After five minutes of awkward conversation, Clipper and Jenny departed for the restaurant.

"I can't believe my dad," Jenny said as they drove away. "When a guy comes over, he turns into a very bad comedian. I think it's his way of hanging onto my childhood. Some guy comes along, meets my dad, and thinks, 'There's no way I'm gonna put up with this man for a long time.'"

"I thought he was nice." Clipper said as he glanced over at her. The nervousness set in again; but luckily for Clipper, Jenny did most of the talking.

"I can't believe how much he likes you. Both times that I had to cancel out on you, he's given me this huge lecture. I mean, its not like I meant to back out. But anyway, when I told him who you were, he turned into this million-questions-a-minute kind of guy. He hated Tim. Couldn't stand him."

"Tim? Is he the guy you, uh—"

"Dated. Right. Dad thought he was way too old for me. He's a freshman at Notre Dame now. We started dating when he was a senior at Western and I was a freshman. Last year, you know. At the end of the year."

"So when did you guys break it off?" Clipper asked, probing the relationship for any signs of life.

"Actually, we tried to keep the relationship going when he went off to school but . . . it never would've worked. I saw him a couple of weeks ago. Dad and Mom both went ballistic."

It relieved Clipper to be in the listener role for a while. Usually he was able to outtalk anyone, but not tonight.

Clipper turned into a parking space at Jaques Seafood Restaurant. He got out of the car slowly and then rushed around to the other side of the car to open the door for Jenny. As he opened the door, he held out his hand to hers. She whispered under her breath, "I'm impressed, Clipper."

"You should be. I never do that for Justin."

Jenny laughed.

"So what did you tell your parents?" Jenny asked.

"I told them that I was going out for a gallon of milk and that I'd be back in about three hours."

"Yeah . . . Right."

Clipper almost flinched when he felt Jenny's fingers curl around his.

Surprise #1: unprovoked hand holding. He was speechless for a minute.

"Everything . . . OK?" Jenny said, smiling.

"Oh . . . Yep. I'd say things are fine. Just fine." He thought to himself, *Man, I do not want to wake up!*

Clipper went back to the subject of his parents. "Seriously, I didn't tell Mom and Dad where we were going. This is our night, and I don't really want them snooping around checking up on me."

"They'd do that?"

"If you only knew. Plus, it takes the mystery out of it. I'd tell them one thing and then another. I like keeping them in the dark. It kind of lets them know that I have a life. Does that make sense?"

Jenny giggled, "I guess so."

"I mean they know about you. They can get nosy sometimes. I'm not exactly the kind of guy who goes out every Friday night. So I'm sure they did their homework," Clipper said smiling. "They've probably found out your Social Security number, your G.P.A., your ties to independent militia groups etc. . . . They're onto you, Jenny, so it's best to not give them a head start."

Jenny laughed.

They walked through the ornate door and to the reception podium. An auburn-haired twentysomething greeted them. "Two?"

"Two." Clipper said, nodding.

The hostess maneuvered them through the crowded restaurant.

"Oh, my gosh. Oh—my—gosh," Clipper said as if he'd just seen the ghost of John Candy.

"What is it, Clipper? What's going on?" Jenny said.

"My mom and dad. They're here," Clipper replied.

Jenny laughed out loud.

"I don't think it's that funny. I can't believe they'd do this."

"I thought you didn't tell them where we'd be," Jenny said, trying to stifle the urge to laugh again.

"I didn't! They must have found out."

"Do they see us?" Jenny asked.

"No. Not yet. They're the couple in the corner booth."

Jenny pushed him in their direction, "Well, let's at least go say hi to them."

"Are you nuts! They want to follow me around, let them find *me*."

Jenny laughed, apparently enjoying Clipper's frustration. After what Clipper thought was a full-scale tour of the restaurant, the hostess finally seated them. Clipper seemed to evolve into a zombie as he sat there stunned at this strange turn of events, while Jenny continued to smile during the lull in the conversation.

"Jenny, would you mind if I go to the restroom really quick?" Clipper said.

"Clipper, I'm your date, not your homeroom teacher. Please, by all means, go to the restroom," she replied playfully.

Clipper made a beeline for the phone booth and dialed his parents' cell phone number.

"Hello?" Clipper's mom answered at the corner booth.

"Very funny, Mom."

"What? Where are you?" she replied.

"I'm at Jaques Seafood."

"You're kidding!"

"No, duh," Clipper said sarcastically.

Clipper could hear her laugh and say to Mr. Hayes. "They're here!"

His dad laughed too, "Let me see that thing." Clipper heard him say, "Clipper, this is exactly what I was talking about. There are really a lot of good reasons to tell us your plans."

"Right," Clipper said with a hint of sarcasm, "You really expect me to believe that this was all a big coincidence."

"Of course. We thought this was way out of your price range. Plus you don't even like seafood. It was a no-brainer. You're the last person I thought we'd see here."

"Jenny loves seafood. You knew. Don't tell me you didn't."

"We didn't know. Hey, there's a cute blonde-haired girl waving at us. That must be Jenny," Mr. Hayes said.

"Well . . . well . . . I guess it's all over but the introductions," Clipper surrendered, then hung up the phone and walked back to his table. "OK," he said with a fake smile, "Let's you and me go meet the family."

After a moment of awkward introductions, Mr. and Mrs. Hayes scooted on out without even ordering. Mr. Hayes told the hostess, "I'm so sorry. We changed our minds. Here's a tip." He handed five dollars to the confused waitress.

"That was quick. I think they were telling the truth. No ambush, just a coincidence," Clipper said.

They sat back down at their table. And for a moment they just sat there looking at each other. Clipper broke the silence. "Thanks for coming."

"Thanks for putting up with my freaky schedule. I thought you would have given up on me after the second time I backed out. But you were persistent. I like that in you. I think you're a really great guy."

Surprise #2: the unprovoked compliment. Clipper once again was speechless.

Nothing more intelligent than the word *duh* came into his mind. *I think you're a really great guy.* The words echoed through his head, sending vibrations all the way down to his toes. Finally, with vocabulary rebooted, he spoke honestly, "Jenny, why'd you come? I mean, I've been—"

"Hey!" A voice spoke out just behind Clipper.

Jenny looked up and smiled. "Garrett! Angela!"

Clipper knew Garrett and Angela from a distance, and being very aware of social ladders, he knew they were several rungs higher than himself.

"Hey, Clip," Garrett said. "This is really a surprise to see you and Jenny. I mean, together. You know, quite a major surprise. Both of you. Here. In the same booth."

Angela was even less merciful in her reaction, "So, Jenny, is this some kind of sociological experiment?"

"You guys are so—" Jenny said, wondering what adjective to use. She shook her head in disgust.

Before she could finish, Garrett jumped in, "So, Jenny, I heard you and Tim were back together."

"Where'd you hear that?" Jenny said contorting her eyebrows and feeling uncomfortable.

"From the horse's mouth. Tim himself." Garrett replied. "He said you're a little skeptical about the whole thing, but he's still got a thing for you; he's still committed."

"It's over, Garrett."

"Quote you on that?" Garrett asked.

"Quote away. Release it to the press. I can tell you that the fat lady has definitely sung," Jenny said flatly.

Clipper drummed his fingers on the table, trying to look comfortable with the whole situation. He felt like a piece of furniture. *One moment I'm about to pour out feelings that I've held back for six months and the next I'm the punch line of a joke from Mr. Popularity.*

As Angela and Garrett continued their enriching conversation, Clipper toyed with the idea of excusing himself. But he decided to just endure it. Finally, they left.

"They're nuts," Jenny said, trying to make light of their encounter with Garrett and Angela.

Clipper looked away.

"They were just joking with you, Clipper," Jenny said.

Clipper was silent.

"OK, they were rude."

More silence.

"Beyond rude," Jenny said.

"No, I just . . . I'm not where they are," Clipper said awkwardly.

"I guess that's why I like you," Jenny said as she reached across the table and grabbed his hand. "That's where I was. Kind of still there. I'm in the brat pack until they say I'm not. They are totally devoid of innocence. They come to parties with fake IDs and condoms. I went to those parties because if you're invited you just go. You know what I mean?"

"Nope. I was never invited," Clipper said half smiling.

"Well, I felt I had to go. I saw them as the best of Summit. That's how I met Tim."

"Speaking of . . ." Clipper interrupted. "Is it over?"

"Yes. Kaput. Over. No more. I could kill him!" Jenny said angrily. "I told him it was over. We agreed and then he goes off telling Garrett that I'm still interested in the relationship. He is such a hypocrite!"

"Hypocrite?"

"Could we just change the subject?" Jenny asked.

"I'll be glad to."

Clipper nervously prayed for something, anything to say that would ease the sudden chill. Finally he spoke. "Let's see, we've kicked Mom and Dad out, cleared up the Tim deal, and we haven't even gotten our entrees yet," Clipper said.

They both smiled, and then laughed.

"I wonder where they are now?" Autumn said to Justin.

Justin, who was driving Autumn and Kandi to his house to watch a movie with a few other friends, shook his head. "Love to know myself. You know, we could just drop in on them at the art show."

"I'm sure he'd love that," Kandi said, cynically.

All three were in the front seat of Justin's old Caprice Classic.

"So, Autumn, how's the project going with Felix?" Kandi asked.

"It's not going."

"What?" Kandi exclaimed.

"He didn't want to do it. Said he was happy the way he was without a high school diploma. I tried, but he got defensive really fast. I couldn't believe it. I mean, I've talked with him about not graduating and how he wished he could have a second chance. But when I offered him the chance, he wouldn't budge."

"So what now?" Justin asked.

"No earthly idea," Autumn replied. "Guess I'll just have to find another project." A few moments passed, then Autumn said, "Maybe that's why he didn't want to do it. Maybe he felt like he was just another project to me."

"I think you're overanalyzing the whole thing," Justin said.

"It's in the genes, I guess. If there's a way to feel guilty about something, I'll find it," Autumn replied.

Justin tapped the steering wheel to the music on the radio and then sighed, "Sure wish I knew how things were going."

"With who?" Kandi asked.

Autumn and Justin said in unison, "Clipper and Jenny!"

The three of them were so caught up in their own speculation they didn't even see Jenny and Clipper passing them on the road. Clipper didn't notice either as he drove Jenny to the Fine Arts Center. He took a rural farm road, Stumberg Lane, a shortcut only native Indianapolis folks would know to take.

"I don't even understand why my Dad stays with Mom," Jenny said. "They've been separated on and off for five years now. Right now it's on. But I'm a pessimist. She'll blow it again, and we'll be back in the same position we were a year ago. I don't get it. It's like Mom has this spirit or personality or something that won't let her stay in one place, with one relationship. And Dad's totally blind to it. He loves her. Period. She has an affair. He blames himself. 'Well, Jenny, I was probably leaving her open to that,' he'll say."

Jenny shook her head and paused. Clipper stayed quiet, not knowing what to say.

"I just want to slap him into reality sometimes," Jenny continued. "I say, 'Are you nuts! She's sleeping around.' I love him for seeing past all that but . . ." Tears pooled in Jenny's eyes. Her countenance changed. "I can't believe I'm doing this to you. You didn't take me out for this."

"Right," Clipper said. *That sounded awful,* he thought. "What I mean is, it's OK. I want to know—I've *wanted* to know about you, Jenny. I want to be there for you."

Clipper wheeled the car to the shoulder of the deserted road.

"What are you doing?" Jenny asked as she wiped her eyes.

"I'm like . . . very compartmentally challenged."

"What's that mean?" Jenny said smiling curiously.

"I can't walk and chew gum at the same time, so I doubt if I can say this and drive."

Jenny laughed lightly as the car behind them whizzed by. Clipper shifted to park, cut the engine, and turned on his hazard lights. "I don't ever want you to think you can't tell me anything. I know I'm not the ultimate guy. I'll never be a Garrett or Tim."

"That's a relief."

"I'll never look like them or sound as cool as they sound. Words don't just roll off my tongue like they do for some people. But I'm good at faithfulness. I do that really well. And I just—"

Jenny placed her hand on his cheek. She moved closer. *What is happening!* Clipper thought and then continued, "I just need you to know that I really . . ." *She's moving closer! You have got to be kidding!! Can we just freeze this moment?!* he thought.

"Really?" Jenny whispered.

"Really." Clipper said with his heart jumping out of his shirt. **Surprise #3: the big surprise.** Their lips met.

A moment later, Jenny embraced him and whispered, "Uh, I didn't plan that one."

"Wow. Me neither. Had no idea. I was just . . . wow."

"Sorry," Jenny said.

"Hey," Clipper said, "It's not . . . well . . . a negative. I don't think I was . . ." She kissed his cheek. "Opposed to the . . . thing. It's just whoa! I mean. I don't know what I mean. Good. Very . . . nice."

"I guess we should go," Jenny said.

"Right. Go. I'll start the car."

"Good idea," Jenny said laughing.

He turned the key and the ignition didn't make a sound.

"Problem?" Jenny asked.

"I am not believing this," Clipper said. He tried it again. Nothing.

"You're kidding," Jenny said.

"I wish I was."

"It won't start?" Jenny asked, and then laughed lightly. "This is really funny. I've heard of some guys trying to do this, but—"

"Dad told me the thing was fixed. The starter."

"The starter?" Jenny asked.

"We had a short in the starter. I guess I can say we still have a short in the starter."

"I definitely have no idea what you are talking about."

"I'm not that much of a mechanic, but I just know that if this happens—" Clipper continued as he reached under the seat on the car and pulled out a hammer. "I take this hammer and klunk on this starter thingy and sometimes it cures the problem. But my dad . . . ah, I can't believe this . . . my dad said it was fixed. A new thingy—but no! It is doing the same old thing. . . . Thanks a lot, Dad."

Clipper got out of the car, opened the hood, and peered into the engine. He thought to himself, *Why does this stuff always happen to me? All I wanted was a semi-flawless night*. Clipper tried "klunking" on the starter, then he hopped back in and tried the ignition. Not a sound. He repeated the process four times but the car refused to respond. It was now cold as a corpse.

"So this really worked?" Jenny asked.

"It did last time," Clipper said nervously.

"Work or not, I'm having fun watching you try," Jenny said smiling.

"I am *so* sorry, Jenny."

"No big deal. The art show can wait."

"So how 'bout a stroll to the gas station."

"There's one around here?"

"It's about a mile, maybe less, just over the hill," Clipper replied.

"Sounds fun."

She grabbed Clipper's hand as he said, "I can't believe you aren't mad."

"Me? I'm having a great night."

Jenny and Clipper walked and talked. They talked about nothing. They talked about everything.

"I'm just going to be up front about this whole thing," Clipper said as the conversation became more relaxed and easy. "Why are you here?"

"Why am I here?" Jenny asked thoughtfully. "Let's see. Why am I here? Hmmm. You know that question could have several different answers."

"Let me clarify," Clipper proposed. "I'm Clipper Hayes. A friendly and yet rather unique-looking guy with average intelligence, 2.6 average to be exact, and a less than average vehicle."

Jenny looked at him and smiled.

Clipper relented. "OK, below average vehicle. Lousy, unreliable vehicle. But you! You are Jenny Elton. Incredibly fun, tons of friends, blonde hair, blue eyes, all the bells and whistles, great to talk to, surely the inspiration of a ton of poetry— half of which I wrote myself this year . . ."

Jenny smiled, "I'm a believer in streams."

"Streams? I don't get it," Clipper said, now curious.

"I hope not. It's *my* term," Jenny said.

"*Your* term?"

"I thought it up this past year. See, I believe that there are people who are just your average ordinary people. They might look great. They might be popular but there is not much under the surface. Under the rock-hard *ex*terior there's just a rock-hard *in*terior. And there are *other* people who seem really nice on the surface but you get close and you'll get hurt. They have this molten lava just below the crust."

"Ouch," Clipper said laughing.

"Does any of this make any sense?" Jenny asked.

"I think so. Keep going," Clipper said and smiled.

"And then there are those people who, well, if you get under the surface of appearance, of words . . . if you go down deep, you'll find a secret . . . stream. A place not very many people see. People just never take the time to look. But you know that it's real. These people might look as dry as a desert but there's a stream that flows, and it's what keeps them alive and it might be what keeps their friends alive. The stream holds on to them. And they hold on to the stream." Jenny looked embarrassed by her sudden philosophical explanation. "I know it sounds goofy."

"It doesn't. I think I understand," Clipper said seriously.

"I know you, Clipper Hayes. There's a current that flows underneath the surface. I don't know where it came from. But it's there."

Autumn's father rarely answered the phone after Autumn had made a sincere plea for him to let her be the designated phone answerer. She was convinced his voice scared away most guys. And the way he answered the phone, "Good evening, Reverend Sanders speaking," announced to everyone who called her that she was a preacher's kid. As if they wouldn't know who he was? Reverend Sanders was the senior pastor of the largest African-American congregation in the city. And his deep bass voice was the giveaway.

"Who do you think they'd mistake you for? Certainly not me or Mom?" Autumn would argue.

Her dad would just smile. "It's just common courtesy," he'd say.

But on this Saturday morning, Autumn was getting dressed in the bathroom, so she gave him telephone clearance.

"Good Morning, Reverend Sanders speaking."

"Dis be Reverend Sanders, whose daughter is Autumn?"

"Yes, it is."

"'Scuse me there fo' callin'. My name is Felix."

"Oh, Felix. Of course, Felix. We met in Ms. Jarvis' office a few weeks ago. How are you doing?"

"I'm doin' well. Yes sir."

"Good."

"I suppose you want to speak to Autumn. I'll get her."

Autumn came out in her bathrobe, with green facial cream on her face and a towel wrapped around her head. Autumn's father cupped his hand over the mouthpiece. "Autumn, are you going to talk to Felix like that?"

Autumn rolled her eyes and slapped her father on the back.

"Honor thy father and thy mother," he said as he laughed.

"Hey, Felix," she said.

"Autumn, I know dat you might have changed your project, so don't feel like I'd be mad if you couldn't but—"

Autumn's eyes lit up, "You'll do it!"

"Dat is if you ain't got nothin' already underway," he said tentatively.

"Ahhh!" Autumn shrieked and jumped, startling her mom and dad, who were sitting at the breakfast table next to her. "That's great! 4:30 today! We've got a lot to do, so come prepared. Actually, you don't have to bring anything. I mean mentally. Just come prepared mentally. Felix? Are you there? Felix?"

"I guess dat's a good kind of excitement, no?" Felix said, a little overwhelmed by Autumn's reaction.

"Yes. Definitely. I'm just so excited that we're going to try this thing together."

"I don't want to mess dis whole thing up." Felix said sheepishly.

"There is no way you can mess it up. This is going to be great. I promise. We'll make it if we both give it 100 percent." Autumn said.

"Hunered and ten. Right?"

"Right. 110 percent. Absolutely."

"So you were stuck on Stumberg Lane with Clipper?" Kandi asked Jenny over the phone that morning. "I don't understand. Run that by me again."

"You don't want to hear everything. It's too unbelievable," Jenny said, clutching the phone while pacing between her computer and bed.

"Believe me. I know Clipper, and I know unbelievable; so lay it on me, Jenny. I can take it. This is way too interesting for you to just tell me the logistics. Did the car just putter out on Stumberg Lane?"

"You're beginning to sound a little like Melissa, Kandi."

"I don't care," Kandi said with growing intensity.

"Truth?"

"Truth."

"We started talking about some stuff." Jenny said thoughtfully, choosing her words carefully.

"Stuff?"

"Stuff . . . and he said he needed to pull over so he could really listen and then when we got ready to go, he turned the key to start the car and nothing happened."

"Nothing?"

"Nothing! Do you need a hearing aid or a new receiver?"

"It's just so . . . weird."

"It was actually kind of fun." Jenny said.

"So that's it. That's all that happened?"

"Well . . . yes."

"Jenny, listen, I'm not trying to pull things out of you and I know that we've only been friends a few weeks, but this is really important to me."

"Why?"

"Cause he's Justin's best friend, and he's like this brother to me and . . ."

"Well, there is this one thing I didn't mention, just a little thing." Jenny said, while wincing just a little.

"OK? One thing," Kandi repeated.

Five seconds of cold, hard silence passed. Then Jenny started—"I . . . I mean we . . . kind of . . . well we did . . . uh . . . we . . . kissed."

No response on the other end from Kandi.

"Hello?" Jenny said.

"Say again?"

"Kandi, I knew I shouldn't have told you but—"

"You kissed who?"

"You really need to get this hearing problem checked out. I kissed him."

"Clipper??"

"No, Kandi, the car—love that car," Jenny said sarcastically, "of course it was Clipper."

"Like on the mouth?"

"Yes. On the mouth."

"Once?"

"Once. And then on the cheek . . . and then halfway to the gas station we uh . . . kissed again. And then when we were waiting, once . . . no twice, while we were waiting. Two small kisses while we were waiting. They were just small, little, short, somewhat non-passionate kisses."

More silence.

"Kandi, would you say something. Anything? Tell me you hate my guts. Anything. Just say something!"

"I'm not angry, Jenny. I'm just stunned. Totally stunned. Totally and completely flabbergasted."

"Kandi. I just kissed him. You're making it sound like I slept with him or something," Jenny said defensively.

"I'm sorry," Kandi responded, trying not to laugh. "And this will stay between me and you. I'll keep this a secret if we can have mutual confidentiality on this whole subject. Clipper would die if he knew I said this to you, but you are the first girl he's ever kissed."

That night, Autumn plopped down in front of the computer at school, where she spent half her time these days. She was one of the few students who had a key to the school and the computer lab. Three teachers counted on her to help with several projects. She found the lab to be a quiet retreat, especially on weekends when everyone in her family was running in a thousand different directions. She had spent the past two hours with Felix, teaching him everything from the basics of multiplication to the Constitution. She reached into her purse and inserted a Zip disk into the Mac. She clicked on the file: *"Life, Theology, and Assorted Thoughts."* She scrolled to the end of the long document, typed in the date, and began a new entry:

May 27th

My first day of tutoring with Felix, and there is lots to be done. If he passes the GED, it will be a miracle of Red Sea proportions. Was I really thinking straight when I came up with this idea? I love Felix, but I've already come to the conclusion that his fourth-grade teacher might have been correct in her assessment of Felix's aptitude. Maybe he can't learn what he needs to learn. He's a very slow reader. He has to think about 2 x 2. He thought the Emancipation Proclamation was a medical procedure! The next session will be a real indication about whether he can really retain some of this stuff. I'll give him a really simple pop quiz that will hopefully build up his confidence. And if he can't answer the questions, maybe I need to think twice about this. His attention span is terrible. Anything that I mention, any offhanded remark that I make reminds him of a story or a joke that he heard. It is nerve-racking! But how will I break the news to him if I decide that it isn't going to work? He has such a low self-image anyway. I don't know what to do. I just hope I can live with myself after this is all over.

Clipper and Jenny went out last night. I'm dying to know what happened. I tried to call him before I went to bed, but he wasn't home yet. I called really late, but since Clipper has his own phone line, I didn't think anything about it. It scared me to death when his mom answered, but she was just walking by his room when the phone rang. She said his dad went to pick them up. I didn't ask her about it, but that makes no sense because Clipper was driving the car. It was 12:15 when I called, and he said his curfew was midnight. My guess is that maybe his dad was out looking for him, but Clipper is Mr. "On-Time" Guy! He goes into a panic if he's late for anything. Plus, he practically had to beg for the car. I called Kandi this morning. I know that she knows something. She was in a rush to get out the door, and she said she'd call me later to tell me what happened with Clipper and Jenny. She knows where I am but she hasn't even beeped me. Is she avoiding me? Clipper's gone to the Y with Justin, and I'm clueless. I hate being in the dark! I'd call Clipper's folks, but if he is on bad terms with them, it'll be really awkward, and it would make me look like a gossip-hungry middle-schooler.

On top of everything else, Troy is now in the hospital and the prognosis is grim. It's hard to believe that this once invincible guy is fighting for his life. I just can't help but think that if we had reached out to him more a few years ago, we could have spared him all this pain. Dad says that it's useless to think that way. He says that we can't blame ourselves for the choices others make. I guess it is just in my nature to second-guess.

Spiritual Lesson of the Day: Life is full of second guesses. These days I'm second-guessing everything. From my motives for helping Felix get his diploma to whether Kandi is avoiding me for some unknown reason. God, teach me to be still and stop reading something into every move my friends make.

"I just don't get it," Clipper said, walking into the dressing room at the Y.

"Get what?" Justin asked, certain his friend's discourse about what happened last night on the date was coming.

"The sauna. How's that supposed to be good for you? It's just stationary sweating in my opinion."

"Oh, excuse me. I thought you were finally going to open up and fill me in on Jenny," Justin said. "I mean, you are just stonewalling me."

"I am *not* stonewalling you. This is just not the right place to talk about what happened last night. People are everywhere. It is personal, you know. I don't want to just go blabbing away in front of a bunch of naked guys how my first date with Jenny went."

"Grab the towel; let's hit the sauna," Justin demanded.

"No," Clipper whined. "Not the sauna. Anything but the sauna!"

"Nobody's in there right now; it's private—you can talk. I promise it's not wired. This is not a matter of national security."

Clipper and Justin sat down just opposite each other in the dimly lit sauna.

"It's sweltering in here," Clipper said, waving his hand in front of his face.

"That's what makes a sauna, a sauna." Justin said, rolling his eyes.

Clipper took great pleasure in finding ways to annoy Justin. Today, withholding information was working well as an excellent annoyance. "I'm not letting you out of here until you tell me what happened," Justin said with a smile.

"I'm talking. I'm talking."

"Go."

"We had a great night. Details are not important, but it was great. We talked. I mean really talked. Not this stand-up comedy routine, not this weather analysis talk. I mean, we talked about real stuff."

"What real stuff? Tell me about the real stuff."

"I can't do that."

"Wow. Real stuff, huh." Justin said, convinced now.

Clipper nodded.

Justin waited a second, and then redirected his interrogation, "So, you don't have to tell me about the details of this conversation but—"

"Let's just say it was heavy-duty conversation, and we never made it to the museum," Clipper said as he lifted his eyebrows slightly.

"Whoa. You talked so much you didn't make it to the museum?"

"Actually, the car broke down again," Clipper said.

"Oh, so the car broke down."

Clipper jumped back in and quickly said, "But even if it hadn't broken down I doubt we would have made it."

"Really?" Justin's head leaned forward.

"See, she got kind of emotionally choked up. You know what I mean."

"Are you serious?"

"As a heart attack, my friend. Don't mention it to her."

"Course not. And . . ."

"Well," Clipper said, then paused looking over at the door to check for movement. "I think I love her," He said tentatively then with more force. "That's exactly it. I love Jenny Elton."

"Whoa. Slow it down a little. We've talked about this kind of stuff before."

"I know, I know, but if *you* were there you would understand. I mean, no offense, I'm glad you weren't there. But if you *had been*, you'd understand."

"No I wouldn't, Clipper. You can't just say that. Not on the first date! Absolutely not. You are totally infatuated. You've never dated anybody more than twice!"

"So what? What do I care? Are the date police gonna walk in an arrest me for premature use of the 'L' word? I can say I love her if I want to. I love Jenny Elton. I love Jenny Elton!!"

The door opened and a man, well into his eighties, walked in. "Mind if I join you?"

"Oh no, not at all." Justin said.

Clipper, wondering if he had heard his embarrassing attempt at an Oscar-winning soliloquy agreed, "Sure, we're just sweating away."

"Thanks," the old man said. He sat close to Clipper. Justin smiled and shook his head. There was a very long, awkward period of silence.

"Oh, to be young and in love," the old man said.

Clipper turned beet red, and Justin bit his tongue to keep from laughing out loud.

They didn't speak again until they were dressed and out of the building. Clipper walked quickly to the car, with Justin trailing right behind him.

"Clip, would you just settle down."

Clipper turned around when he got to the car door and pulled out his keys, "Why is it that I'm OK when I'm only *wishing* that I had some . . . some semblance of a social life. Wait . . . this is bigger than social. Why is it that when I meet the girl and think that she might, just *might,* be the one I'm going to have a very strong commitment—"

"Don't say that, Clipper!"

"There you go again, Justin. I can't even complete a sentence without you butting in on me. You are driving me nuts!"

Justin responded quickly, "Clipper, don't you remember last fall when we made a commitment to watch out for each other and make sure that neither one of us went over the deep end about anything or anyone."

"This is not one of those times. I thought you'd be excited

about this. And instead you're like 'Whoa—let's not get too happy, now. Let's not get too excited about it.' What is your deal, man? I haven't popped the question."

"That's good," Justin said.

"As if I would! Sheesh!"

"Well, you told her you love her."

"No! You aren't even listening," Clipper said, his eyes animated and wide open. "I told *you* I love her. Talk about jumping to conclusions! You know what I think your problem is?"

"Nope, but I'm sure you're going tell me," Justin said under his breath.

"I think you might be just a bit jealous that your relationship with Kandi doesn't have that kind of spark."

"Don't go there, Clipper. Let's just drop it."

"Fine with me," Clipper said as he fiddled with his keys to unlock the driver's side. "I'm fine, Justin. Just fine. I haven't been better. I see things clearer. I have more confidence. I'm wiser—"

Justin interrupted, "And you're trying to unlock somebody else's car."

School ended and the four friends who seemed inseparable since April, grew further apart. Justin heeded Clipper's warning to back off. They still worked together at the BurgeRama, but things between them changed.

Kandi gave Clipper almost the same words of caution that Justin had given him. She said, "I just don't want to see you get hurt."

"Why does everybody want to play counselor with me?" Clipper said, walking away and shaking his head. He turned back around "I can't believe you two won't trust me!"

Autumn consumed herself in her newest project: Felix. And she sensed Kandi's concern that she might be giving Felix some false hopes on reaching an unreachable goal. Kandi brought it up once but backed off quickly.

In early June, Autumn wrote:

It's crazy. We've been through so much in the past few months. We've seen friends die in car wrecks, we've been falsely accused, almost expelled and now all of a sudden, everything's OK. Except it's not OK. We're all really edgy. We should just sit down and talk about it or maybe go out together and just have fun. But we're all consumed. It's like we're living separate lives. It's nobody's fault, and yet it's everybody's fault.

Sixteen students squeezed into the small journalism lab for Mrs. Tisdale's annual Summit High yearbook team summer work meeting. The lab contained a few art tables, large tables and stools, and computers with oversized monitors. Windows spanned the outside wall, which looked out on student parking. As Tisdale droned on about yearbook ideas and deadlines, Melissa quietly drilled Jenny.

"So, the Clipper thing's not over?" Melissa asked.

"You treat every relationship in life like some kind of TV show that begins and, thirty minutes later, ends," Jenny said.

"I like to think of it as a soap opera,"

"We've been out a few times. He's sweet."

"So's Barney," Melissa said with a quiet laugh.

"He's sent me flowers twice. My dad thinks he's great. We're really close friends."

"Is this a, like, rebound thing?"

"No, Melissa. Tim was history a long time before Clipper."

"Then," Melissa paused as if not knowing what to say, "Why?"

"You are too much," Jenny whispered. "You think everything is dependent on some almighty social scale. You are too busy watching other people live their lives to have any time whatsoever to live your own!"

Melissa ignored the comment and steered back to the Clipper issue. "I'm still having trouble deciding if you two are dating or just hanging out because—"

"Good. I hope I can keep you wondering."

Melissa kept on, "Because I saw something that night you went out for the first time."

"What?" Jenny whispered intensely.

"I didn't ask you about it because I really couldn't imagine it being what it looked like."

"What are you talking about?" Jenny was now genuinely curious and little self-conscious.

"I saw something that made me think you didn't go to the art museum like you said you did. By the way, did you?" Melissa asked.

Jenny rolled her eyes, "No, ma'am, we didn't make it to the art museum. Don't tell me you hired a private detective to scope the place out."

"Good guess, but no."

"Carla and I were going down Stumberg Lane, and we saw Clipper's car on the side of the road. We slowed down thinking you two might need help. But we couldn't see anything. The windows were, like . . . steamed."

"You are *so* wrong," Jenny said as she grabbed her notebook and purse.

Mrs. Tisdale, seeing Jenny stand up to leave, stopped her lecture midsentence. "Girls? Is there a problem?"

"Uh, no," Jenny said. "I'm sorry, I'm not really feeling very good—"

Melissa jumped in, "And I'm, like, helping her. In the bathroom. Sorta. Cuz, like she said, she's not, like, feeling good. I mean . . . well, I'm going to help her. I'll be right back."

The students groaned. Typical Melissa response.

Jenny hurried to the girls room. She opened one of the stalls, fell to her knees, and regurgitated. Melissa watched in total shock.

"You really are sick, aren't you."

"Yes, I'm sick," Jenny said, still bent over the toilet.

"This isn't some kind of diet purging thing is it? Cuz that's not good. I saw this show on 'Dateline' where—"

"Would you just shut up!" Jenny screamed.

"Pardon moi," Melissa said dramatically.

"You don't ever quit, do you?" Jenny said. "I'm in here puking my guts out, and you're telling me about some news story."

"Oops," Melissa said, shrugging her shoulders.

"Oops? That's all you can say? Oops?"

"OK, OK, I'm sorry."

"No, Melissa, I didn't go parking with Clipper instead of going to the museum. And I am not—"

The door opened. And another student walked in. "Is everything OK?"

"No," Jenny said. "Everything's not OK. I'm sick and I need to get home."

"Do you need me to—" the girl said.

"Please. Thanks. That'd be great."

Jenny left with the other student without a backward glance at Melissa.

Melissa walked back into the meeting looking flustered. Mrs. Tisdale was still going over deadlines and rules. "It is absolutely imperative that by February all photos—Melissa, is everything all right with Jenny?"

"She's gone home with Chelsea."

"Could you make sure she gets the handouts?"

"Sure," Melissa mumbled.

Melissa returned to the table in the back of the room where she and Jenny were sitting before they left for the bathroom. She scooted back to her place and picked up the handouts. Underneath the newly copied forms and schedules was a journal. She remembered Jenny walking in with the book and being curious about what was in it. She picked it up and thumbed through it. Two paragraphs were written on the first page. Melissa wondered if the two paragraphs were the continuation of another journal because it started so abruptly. She closed the book quickly and scoped out the room, checking the door to see if Jenny was coming back for it, and then looked out the window. She saw Chelsea's car pulling out of the parking lot with Jenny inside, so Melissa opened the journal again and read while Mrs. Tisdale droned on about breaking the group into committees.

"I took the test and it showed positive. Why did I do it? Mom and Dad are going to go freak out when I tell them. If I tell

*them. I don't even know. I really believe I could get this whole
thing taken care of and forget about it. But I'm scared. I've
had nightmares about it. I've lost either way. I remember
all those times they'd rag on me about guys and I thought I
was so—"*

The journal entry ended abruptly. Her mouth agape,
Melissa looked up again, knowing any second Jenny could
return once she realized she had left the journal. She read the
paragraph again, and then once more, trying to digest it, even
memorize it. She looked out the window and, as expected, the
car was back and Jenny ran back to the building. Melissa slid
out toward the door again.

"Melissa," Mrs. Tisdale said with obvious aggravation, "I
wish you would make up your mind! In or out."

"It's this," Melissa said waving the journal, "Jenny left this
book and she's coming back and—"

"OK. OK." Tisdale said, rolling her eyes.

Jenny walked quickly to the entrance and met Melissa.

"You found it," Jenny said between breaths.

"Yeah, I saw you come in with it, and then when I went
back in I—"

"Did you read it?" Jenny asked.

"Me? Read what?" Melissa said innocently.

"What's in the book?"

"I thumbed through it but . . . uh . . . didn't see anything
in it," Melissa lied.

"Great," Jenny said. She couldn't hide her relief. Jenny
instinctively hugged her.

"What's that? I thought you were hacked off."

"Gotta go," Jenny said as she turned to leave.

Down the hall in the computer lab, Felix and Autumn waded through a sample test Autumn bought at the bookstore. Felix sailed through the mathematics section successfully, but he failed miserably on the history, chemistry, science, literature, and reading comprehension sections.

"Dis ain't no use, no how."

"We still have five weeks before the exam. Don't give up so fast," Autumn said assertively.

"But you gonna miss out on de credits fo college if I don't do no good," Felix said, trying to convince her to give up.

"Don't worry about me, Felix. If we don't pass, then we don't pass."

"You means we fail. I fail."

"Don't say that word."

"Whatchu mean?"

"Fail. Don't say *fail*. If you just keep looking at all the things you don't know, you'll never succeed."

"But—" Felix tried to interject.

"Look at the results on the math; they're *passing* scores. We just have to knock out the other areas."

"Dis is too much learnin', Autumn. Too much," Felix got up and walked to the door.

"Fine," Autumn said angrily. "You want to give up, then go ahead. But I believe you can do this."

Felix stopped and turned around.

Autumn continued, "Felix, your whole life has been a series of 'no trespassing' signs."

"Whatchu saying there?"

"I'm saying that everybody—your bosses, your parents, your teachers—everybody has told you you can't do this or that. All your life you've heard how helpless you are. But I know you aren't. You just need to give yourself a chance, Felix! This is your chance to prove to everybody that you really can do something, something they never thought you could do."

Felix stood still for a moment, and then walked out.

"I don't know what the deal is with everybody," Kandi said to Autumn as they strolled through a nearly empty mall one rainy Thursday night. "Must be a psychological relapse or something."

"You've lost me. What are you talking about?"

"I mean, look at all the stuff we've been through," Kandi explained. "I think we're all really tired, and then add to it that Troy's losing weight and getting weaker. It's a lot of stress. And now we're all out of school, working on our own issues. Justin and I are in a rut. You're trying to finish this project with Felix."

"And Clipper's totally flipped out over Jenny," Autumn said.

They stopped when they heard a familiar voice yell, "Hey!"

They turned around to see Melissa carrying four shoe boxes in an oversized plastic bag. Kandi and Autumn smiled politely as they greeted her. They could tell they were about to hear some news and commentary simply by the way Melissa excitedly scooted over to them.

"Looks like some serious shopping," Autumn said to Melissa.

"Shoes Unlimited was like a madhouse two hours ago," Melissa replied.

"Really?" Kandi said.

"Like, everything was, like, two for one. I got new pumps and some Reeboks, and some of these thong thingys."

"So three pairs?" Autumn asked.

"Nope, eight. I had to leave these in the store for a while. Too much to carry all at once. You know, they could, like, make some major bucks if they had those rental carts like they do at the airport, where you pay a buck and well, you know—"

"Sounds like an idea all right." Autumn said.

"So Kandi, where's Justin?" Melissa asked.

"Justin who?" Kandi joked. "Seriously, he's working."

"Oh yeah. BurgeRama," Melissa said. "With Clipper?"

"Don't know," Kandi said.

"Think so." Autumn said.

"Boy, things are getting hot and heavy between Clipper and Jenny, huh?" Melissa said.

"I don't know," Autumn said, "When *I* talk to Jenny, she sounds like she's talking about her brother."

"I guess she's a good actress," Melissa said, "and maybe Clipper is wild about her because the relationship has gone just about as far as it could possibly go," Melissa said.

Kandi furrowed her brow and gestured with her hand for Melissa to continue. Melissa raised her eyebrows, offering no more information. Autumn and Kandi looked at each other in bewilderment. But they weren't going to let that comment rest without some sort of explanation. They demanded more.

"Come on, Melissa. What's the deal?" Kandi asked.

"Don't play games with me. You two are pretty close to them. I'm sure you've already heard about Clipper and Jenny's situation."

"I think not," Autumn said, smiling, with a fair amount of confusion.

Kandi shifted her weight and thought out loud. "I'm sure Justin hasn't told you anything. And we talk to Clipper almost every day. We all know he really likes her," Kandi said to Melissa.

"Oh, I think the relationship is a little more than that," Melissa said, throwing out another piece of juicy verbal bait.

Kandi had heard enough, "Melissa, would you stop the charades and tell us what you're saying?!"

"All I'm saying is that they are really getting physical, and I don't mean in a Gatorade kind of way."

"Physical?" Autumn said, totally stunned. "You mean like kissing, right?"

Melissa laughed, "A little more than a kiss."

"I don't know where you get your information, but that is impossible."

"I know Clipper, Melissa," Kandi said. "And that's just not true. Maybe a kiss. Maybe a hug, but not—"

"More than a kiss. More than a hug," Melissa clarified unemotionally.

"What makes you the expert on this relationship? Can't you just keep out of this?" Autumn said angrily.

"I know what I saw," Melissa said, matching Autumn's intensity.

"What, for crying out loud, did you see?" Kandi demanded.

"I was driving down Stumberg Lane one night," Melissa explained. "In fact, the first time they went out. I remember because we had talked about it beforehand. Anyway, when I was driving down Stumberg that night, I, like, saw Clipper's car off the road. I thought maybe something was wrong, but once I got close enough to really see, I backed out of there fast."

"So, what did you see?" Autumn asked.

"Oh come on, Autumn. You're not that stupid."

"Melissa," Kandi said. "This is *such* old news."

Autumn jumped in, "Clipper's car wouldn't start."

"Then why did they stop the car?" Melissa countered.

"Because they wanted to talk for a second. That's what he told us, and I believe it," Kandi said.

"You two are so naive. They wanted to *talk*? Sounds like a place to use more body *language* than words, if you know what I mean," Melissa said smiling.

"That's not even funny," Kandi said angrily.

"It's gotten a lot worse than that. I know they're sleeping together. I can't tell you how, but the evidence I have would stand up in a court of law," Melissa said matter-of-factly.

"The court of Sally Jesse?"

"Fine. Fine with me . . ." Melissa said as she began to back off. "Live in denial. See if I care. I even know they weren't using any kind of protection."

"What!" Autumn said, obviously shocked and embarrassed.

"Would you just SHUT UP!" Kandi said angrily.

"Fine, Pollyanna," Melissa said as she walked away.

"It's a good thing she left," Autumn fumed. "I was about to cram a couple of those shoe boxes up her nose."

Clipper was on top of the world for the few weeks he and Jenny were together. Though they went out only a few times, their relationship deepened. They spent lots of time on the phone, and Clipper kept the florist busy. Then Jenny left with her family on a dreaded 700-mile, five-day visit to distant relatives. Clipper was intolerable to his friends, who described him as "one lovesick puppy." The guy wrote poetry, made a screen saver of her picture for his computer, and put an incessant number of E-mails in her in box.

Around sunset on the fourth day of Jenny's absence, Clipper was helping his dad install a motion-sensitive light on the front porch when a car pulled up to their curb. Jenny got out and the car drove off. Clipper, facing the house, didn't notice anything, but his dad did.

"Hey, Jenny," Mr. Hayes said.

"Oh, yeah, right Dad. As if you haven't done that a thousand times this week," Clipper said.

"Hi, Clipper." Jenny said.

Clipper jerked around, lost his balance, and fell off the ladder. Scrambling to his feet, he laughed awkwardly and greeted Jenny with a "Dad's watching" type hug. "You're back early. I thought you were going to be back tomorrow night."

"We got a little weary of sleeping on couches and foam mattresses, so we cut it short," she said and then whispered, "I missed you."

"Uh, Dad, mind if I—"

"You'll do anything to get out of work," Mr. Hayes said smiling, "Be careful around the ladder though, son. Wouldn't want anyone to get hurt."

Clipper gritted his teeth and growled playfully. He and Jenny walked to the back of the house. "I am so glad the reunion tour got out short. I was starting to get the shakes and go into withdrawals. By the way, I think I overloaded your in-box. After about the twenty-sixth E-mail, I started getting these 'unable to deliver' notifications. Sorry. I was just going nuts, and if I E-mailed you it was kind of like you weren't gone. I tried calling you at your grandmother's house, but you weren't there, and then I had to work all day, and when I got back it was 10:30, which would have been even later due to the time zone, and I decided it wouldn't be kosher to wake your grandma up. But I wanted to. I went all the way up to the last number, and then I stopped myself. I thought, this is stupid. Why build a lousy reputation with the family by calling during Letterman. So then I called you the next morning, and I overslept and you had already left."

Jenny didn't respond to his overblown, verbose mono-
logue. Her mood was dark, and she was very quiet as they sat
down on the porch swing.

Clipper looked at her and said, "I'm sorry, I've just been rat-
tling on and on and haven't let you get a word in edgewise."

"It's not you," Jenny said. "I'm sorry. I'm just going through
a really . . . I just . . . I don't know what to say, but it isn't your
fault." Clipper said nothing, but wondered where the conversation was going.

Jenny looked over at him, then looked away and said the
words Clipper feared. "I think it might be best for you if we
stopped dating."

"OK," Clipper said, trying to admit the power of the statement. His forehead felt as if it were in a vice, and he was afraid
his heart would explode.

Jenny finally continued, "I still want to be with you, but I
am dealing with so much stuff personally that I don't think I
can be a real participant in a relationship right now."

"Why?" Clipper asked. His face was pale.

"It is nothing that you did. OK? Nothing. I'm just having a
really tough time with myself," Jenny said as a tear rolled down
her cheek. "I am just in so much . . . pain."

"Maybe I could help you work through it," Clipper said.

Jenny's chin quivered.

"What is it, Jenny?"

"I can't tell you that."

"But it's not going to change how I feel about you. Is it
your parents?"

"Clipper, you told me before I left that you loved me, that

you cared for me more than you could imagine anybody caring for anyone. And if you do still care for me . . ." she paused and looked at him.

"No *ifs*. I do," Clipper interrupted as he fought back tears.

"If you still care, I just need you to either be patient with me or forget me completely because I can't . . . I can't function normally, like I have been. I am just hurting. Clipper, you are a great, great guy. And you shouldn't—"

"I should," Clipper interrupted again.

"I know I'm asking a lot of you."

"I don't want it like this. I don't even know what *this* is yet. But I'll do it."

"Clipper, I know you pray," Jenny said hesitantly.

Clipper looked back at her, surprised by the statement.

Jenny continued, "I guess you believe prayer really works?"

"I do," Clipper said solemnly.

"Could you—would you pray?" Jenny broke down again. "For me? Because I am really hurting. I hurt so bad, Clipper. I don't think I can stand the pain anymore."

"Jenny! Why? Tell me why."

"I can't. I just can't," she said through tears. There was another long minute of silence. Then Jenny said, "Can you give me a ride home?"

"Sure."

They walked to Clipper's car without another word. Clipper drove. Jenny rested her head against the door and wiped her tears with the back of her hand. Clipper's mind raced in a thousand different directions as they traveled across the busy intersections of the Indianapolis suburb.

When Clipper pulled up to Jenny's house he put the car in park, and opened his door to walk her to the door.

"Don't," Jenny said. She got out of the car on her own. She walked away without looking back.

Clipper closed his door and wept, placing his forehead on the steering wheel. After a moment he shifted the car back into drive and went home. He parked the car in the driveway, opened the door, and got out. Then, driven by an inner source, he began to run. He ran with no destination—out of the subdivision and down a winding rural road in the humid night air.

An hour later, exhausted and drenched with sweat, Clipper walked into his house. "Where did you go?" his dad asked with concern.

"I can't talk about it right now."

"Something happened with Jenny?"

Clipper nodded.

"Justin called," Clipper's mom said. "He said you need to call him on his dad's cell phone right away. He's out looking for you."

Clipper took the slip of paper with the cell phone number and punched in the digits.

Justin answered on the first ring, "Hello."

"It's me."

"Where've you been? I've been looking all over for you."

"It's a long story, Justin."

"Troy's parents called. They asked us to get to the hospital right away. Troy asked for us. Sounds like he won't make it through the night."

"I'll meet you at the hospital."

"No, Clipper, I just pulled into your driveway. Can you come now?"

"I'll be right out."

Troy, the all-state guard on the school basketball team, symbolized success at Summit High. He had always made everything look easy. But he partied his way into oblivion. Popular, talented, and attractive, he surely would have been voted "Most Likely to Succeed" if he hadn't contracted the AIDS virus. Instead, with an unlikely future, he had graciously accepted the school award for "Most Courageous." The virus had brought Troy to his knees. And there he had discovered a new source of hope through Jesus Christ.

When Justin and Clipper arrived, they were greeted by Troy's parents and Shawn, their youth minister. Both boys could see the desperation in everyone's eyes. Troy was wearing an oxygen mask and was surrounded by monitors and tubes. He gestured for his mom to take the mask off. She hesitated, but at his insistence, she cooperated.

"Some mess I've gotten myself into, huh, Justin?" Troy said. His speech was slurred as he labored to breathe.

"You don't have to talk, Troy," Justin replied.

"I do," Troy said sincerely.

Shawn suggested that Troy's folks leave with him while the three talked. Troy's mom kissed his cheek and walked out of the room with Shawn and Troy's father. "They've been here for two days," Troy labored over the words. "They know it's serious, and I know it too. They can't control my temp, and I'm having trouble breathing. Heard a nurse say to my doctor last night when she thought I was asleep, 'Amazing kid. He's still alive.' But I can't—" he coughed, "I can't fight much longer."

Clipper, still reeling from Jenny's visit, wiped his eyes with the sleeve of his shirt. At that moment, it felt like darkness covered everything in his life.

"You know, my greatest fear is that I'll be forgotten," Troy said quietly. "That the world will go on and . . . and I'll be just another statistic," he finished, gasping painfully for air.

Justin shook his head, "No way, man. We'll never forget you. You just stay strong and you'll—"

Troy cut him off. "No, it's past that."

Justin and Clipper didn't know what to say.

Clipper reached out his hand to Troy. Troy grabbed it tightly, smiled, and said, "I used to rag on you like nobody's business."

"Yeah, Troy," Clipper said as he choked on a tear. "You sure did. You used to drive me nuts."

"I'm sorry, Clip."

"Don't be."

"I did it because I was jealous of your spirit," Troy explained. "The unconquerable Clipper . . ."

"What?" Clipper said, surprised by the remark.

"You had so much riding against you . . . but you . . . took it . . . took it on like . . ." he tried to take a deep breath and ended up coughing.

"I'm not strong," Clipper admitted through tears.

"You don't . . . even . . . know it, do you?" Troy said. "I'm going . . . I'm going to be all right. Isn't that right, Justin?"

"You're gonna be fine," Justin replied with a whisper.

Troy smiled. "He's here."

"Who?" Justin asked. Justin and Clipper looked at each other strangely and then looked back at Troy. Their friend's eyes had fallen shut and his breathing became more peaceful. The doctor returned to the room and took stock of the situation. At 8:26 Troy slipped into a coma. At 5:30 the next morning, Troy died.

10

Two days later Autumn finally returned to her computer journal.

Just back from Troy's funeral. Grove Community Church was packed. I really don't need to write this because I'm sure I'll always remember today. So many sad moments. So many "what ifs." Troy spent his last days fighting a losing battle. I never knew him that well. We probably only talked a couple of times after he got AIDS. Life seems so unfair. Tonight it seems cruel, uncaring, and blind to redemption. I wish there was a way for a person not to face consequences of their lives after they've turned to Christ, but that's not the way it works most of the time. The scars remain. The death of Troy seemed to bring us all together as friends. All except for Clipper. Clipper seemed to be in his own world hardly saying two words when we went out to eat after the funeral. Actually none of us said much. We were so drained, it was a task simply to chew our food. How did all of us become so close to Troy? He was so "anti us" before this disease. He hated everything we were about, and then he started to die and the burden of his dying fell on us. Lester, Toby, Garrett, Carla . . . all those friends of his that he partied with just dropped out of his life. I couldn't believe it. Lester didn't visit him in the hospital or even show for the funeral. I'm glad that we were able to hold his hand through this ordeal. It changed us, I'm sure. Life is indeed but a breath. But it's hard to see the joy tonight. Tonight brings no comfort.

Kandi and I quit working at the BurgeRama. I miss it, but my work load with Project Felix is taking up most of my free time. The project's been very frustrating, but he's making progress. It reminds me of the haiku, "Oh snail. Climb Mount Kilamanjaro. But slowly.":-)

I'm hearing some strange stories about Clipper and Jenny. Don't know if I should tell him what I'm hearing. I'm afraid he'd think that I thought they had some validity if I mentioned them. Plus he seems to be putting up a major wall. A few weeks ago I warned him about not taking the thing with Jenny too fast and for the first time since I've known him, he blew up. Now I'm hearing these stories and I think, "Me? Tell him? No way." But he hasn't ever faced this kind of temptation before as far as I know, and he could stumble so easily on the sex issue. I wonder if he hasn't already stumbled. We are all losing connections as friends.

Lord, help us reunite as friends. We are all tired and down-trodden. Protect Clipper from ridicule and give me the right words to say. And if possible, could you lend Felix a few more brain cells?

c—H—ɔ

"I'm really looking forward to the student conference," Clipper said.

"Me too," Justin agreed as he refilled the paper towels in the men's room at the BurgeRama. Clipper leaned over the sink, shining the faucet with a rag and staring at his distorted reflection.

"I'm just sort of sick of this place."

"Did you invite Jenny?" Justin asked.

"No. I couldn't."

"Why not? You could have invited her just as a friend."

"I don't want to talk about it," Clipper said evasively.

"So when *are* we going to talk about it?" Justin asked.

"Justin, it's something that I don't want to discuss with you now," Clipper said with a hint of calm aggravation in his voice.

"When has there ever, I mean *ever,* been a time when we withheld information from each other?" Justin asked.

"What are you and Kandi doing tonight?" Clipper asked.

"Clipper! Don't act like you didn't hear me. What is the deal?" Justin demanded.

"You want to know what the deal is? I'll tell you what the deal is. I don't know. There. I know less about Jenny than I did before we dated a few times. Look, I am clueless. Did you hear me? Clueless about her."

"What happened? Are you two . . . over?"

"I don't know," Clipper replied.

"What do you mean you don't know?"

"I just don't know. We talked. She said she wanted me to

forget about the relationship—or something to that affect. I don't really remember what she said. She started talking and then crying and my eyes kinda glazed over. I couldn't even listen. It was like her mouth was moving, but my mind was on mute. Does that make any sense to you whatsoever?" Clipper was almost yelling now.

Justin shrugged and Clipper continued, "All I heard was that she needed space. I gave her that, then Troy died, and we've been so busy helping everybody through all that stuff that, well, it's been something that's helped me keep my mind away from what she said. Whatever *that* was. Jenny hasn't said anything since. She hasn't called."

"Have you called *her*?" Justin asked.

"You aren't listening, Justin. She asked me to give her some space."

Justin smiled slightly. "I've asked you to give *me* some space, and you still called *me*."

Clipper shook his head. "This is a girl, Justin."

"So you're just gonna let her go without even knowing why?" Justin asked.

"I'm not you, Justin. I can't do that. I'm not that brave. Dang, it took me five months to say hello to her. Do you think I'm actually capable of pulling off some Oscar-winning love scene? Plus I really *don't* want to hear her reasons for—"

A customer walked into the bathroom and the conversation stopped immediately.

"It's all yours," Justin said to the middle-aged patron in a polite, business-like manner. They grabbed the cleaning supplies and walked back into the dining room.

Clipper continued in a more intense voice, "I really don't want to know why she doesn't want me around. I don't think I could take it. I really don't. She'd just confirm every suspicion I already had. She'd probably say, 'Clipper, you are a really nice guy with a great personality, but this relationship has gone far enough. I really just want to be friends. Distant, wave-across-the-hall type friends.'"

Justin pointed his finger into Clipper's boney sternum, "You don't know that."

Their manager stepped between them. "Guys. Guys . . . Look it's slow right now and it sounds like you really need to talk. I could hear you all the way back at the grill. Why don't you take fifteen minutes to work this thing out, and then concentrate on burgers the rest of the shift."

Clipper and Justin walked outside where the sun slowly slipped behind the skyline. "Justin, I guess the point I'm trying to make is, you think I can do what you can do. You don't get nervous about this stuff, and I do. And plus, she wants space."

Another student from Summit High walked toward the entrance of the BurgeRama a few feet from Justin and Clipper.

"Hey dudes," the student said cheerfully. Once their eyes adjusted to the glare from the sun, they recognized Jeff Langley, a JV basketball team member at Summit. He knew Justin and Clipper but rarely talked with them. He teetered socially between the jocks and the grunge guys at Summit. He was a jovial fellow, totally and completely living life for the fun of it. "Clipper! How's it goin', dude?"

"Great , Jeff," Clipper replied automatically without smiling. "How's your summer?"

"Cool."

"Great."

"I just have to say that you are one major dude on campus," Jeff said.

"Uh, thanks, I guess," Clipper said hesitantly.

"I mean, sleeping with Jenny Elton. What a major score!" Jeff said, winking.

"WHAT?!" Clipper yelled, and then took a big step toward Jeff.

Justin grabbed Clipper's arm to prevent a rash reaction.

Jeff lifted his hands up in the air. "Whoa, like, I guess I was wrong."

"You guessed right. Where did you hear that?" Justin said.

"Can't remember. Just heard it, you know . . . around."

"Where?!" Clipper added, talking another step toward Jeff.

"Gotta go." Jeff backed up, quickly heading back to his car.

"What was that all about?" Clipper asked, pacing the pavement of the BurgeRama. "Who do they think I am? That's the last thing I thought I'd ever be accused of."

"Come on, Clipper," Justin said. "Forget it."

"I can't forget that. You really expect me to go back in there and forget that Jeff Langley, of all people, *Jeff* gets word that I'm supposedly sleeping with Jenny. If he's heard that rumor, everybody else has heard it too." Clipper stopped and looked up at Justin as if a thought just entered his mind. "Have you?"

Justin turned away from him.

Clipper asked again, "Have you heard that rumor?"

Justin exhaled and then looked Clipper in the eyes, "I didn't believe it was true."

"But you heard it."

"I heard it, and I defended you because I knew that it wasn't true. I knew you wouldn't, couldn't do it. And I didn't want to tell you what they were saying because I knew that you were having a tough enough time right now without me breaking the news to you that people were saying these things behind your back."

"You didn't think I could handle it," Clipper said factually.

"Clipper."

"So you didn't want to tell me," Clipper said in shock. He bent over, feeling like he'd had the wind knocked out of him.

"Truthfully, no. I didn't want you to get hurt. When you told me that you and Jenny cut it off, I felt like it would all blow over, and they would see that it wasn't true."

"They? Who's they? Who told you?"

"Kandi told me that some others had told her," Justin said tentatively.

"Others?" Clipper said as he stood up straight again. His mind reeled. He became visibly pale and suddenly ran over to the outside trash can and vomited.

Justin followed him and stopped a good five yards away.

"I'm sick," Clipper stated.

"Yeah. You are. I agree," Justin said.

"Tell 'em I'm sick."

"I'll tell them." Justin said. He tried to think of something to say to Clipper about the rumor. "Clipper, nobody believes it."

"Jeff did. You heard that yourself. He believed it, and others must believe it too," Clipper said.

"They just talk. They don't have anything better to do. I

think you're the one who said that some people talk about others because they don't have a life worth living themselves."

"This is sacred stuff, Justin," Clipper said still clutching the garbage can.

"I know," Justin said.

"What am I supposed to do? Do I just ignore it?"

Justin paused before answering. "You could."

"Should I try to trace this whole thing down to one source?"

Justin shook his head, "You know it doesn't work that way. Stories change so much from day to day. People just pass them around and add their own slant and—"

Before Justin could finish the sentence, Clipper reached for his car keys and headed for his car. As he drove away, he wondered how life could become any more complicated and tragic than it had that week. *No wonder friendships seemed strained and awkward,* he thought. *No wonder Autumn, Kandi, and Justin seemed uneasy about my relationship with Jenny. But why didn't they come to me? Did they stand up for me when they heard all of this, or did they savor each morsel of the story? Did they eagerly await new information from the unnamed source? What is it that they aren't telling me?*

Tears welled up in his eyes as he thought about the public commitment he had made two years ago to remain sexually pure for his future marriage partner. It seemed as if they all thought he'd willingly torn this important commitment to shreds.

Clipper stewed for two days. He rarely left the house or answered the phone. Finally Justin showed up while Clipper was outside pounding the ball on the driveway and shooting free throws. The activity provided an escape from his present situation. It consumed his consciousness as he endured the 100-degree heat wave. He didn't notice Justin until his friend spoke.

"So you've decided not to go to the youth conference?" Justin asked as Clipper flinched.

"Right," Clipper said tersely.

"But you've already put down the money to go," Justin exclaimed.

"Yeah. Too bad. Never see those bucks again."

"You've got to go to this conference. It'll get your mind off some of this junk. It will get your focus back on what's really important," Justin said.

Clipper picked up the dribble and then shot the ball at the chalk mark. "Are you saying that I'm *not* focused on the right things?" Clipper accused.

"I'm just saying that I think going would do you lots of good."

Clipper didn't respond. He grabbed the ball and shot again.

Justin again spoke up, "I just want you to go. Forget about girls for a while."

"You kill me sometimes, Justin. You say it's about time for me to forget about girls, and I know Kandi will be right there with you the whole time. I do have a life outside your shadow. You always think you know what's right and that I'm some sort of—I don't know—imbecile who can't survive without your wisdom."

"I really wish you would stop judging me," Justin said.

"Well, forget YOU! Forget you!" Clipper said loudly.

"I don't believe this."

"Believe it." Clipper shot back.

"I haven't, in all the years I've known you, tried to force-feed my opinions down your throat. And now you have the gall to shove your finger in my face—"

"Who's judging who?" Clipper interrupted with intensity. "You're the one who came here to lay down the guilt trip."

"I'm not trying to make you feel guilty. I'm just coming as a friend to ask you . . . OK, to beg you to go with us. It's already been paid for, and I think it would do us all some good to be together. We've been through a lot of junk the past few days with Troy's death and this Jenny business. If I told you I'd cool it with Kandi while I'm there, would that—"

Clipper interrupted, "No. It wouldn't change my mind, Justin. I just don't want to go. I appreciate the thought, but I am staying here."

"Why are you so angry with me?" Justin asked.

"Why do you feel like everything has to do with you? Could it be that I might have a life outside of my friendship with Mr. Everything?" Clipper said as he dropped the ball.

"That's low, Clipper, and you know it."

"I am so sick," Clipper said kicking the ball on the word *sick,* "of this weird, unfair, the-joke's-on-me life! AIDS, suicide, weirdos, conniving teachers, gossips. I just want to scream!"

"Then scream!" Justin demanded.

"AAAHHHH!" Clipper screamed and rammed the basketball goal pole with his hand.

"Feel better?"

"Not exactly." Clipper replied, smarting from the foolish self-inflicted pain.

"So you'll go?"

"No. I'm not going, and please don't ask me that again," Clipper said, believing it would take more than a three-day spiritual fix to get him out of this philosophical funk.

Instead of going to the National Impact Student Conference, Clipper spent three days in almost total isolation. He zoned out on life, watching old movies, reading, and playing basketball by himself in the backyard. His parents knew something was up, but they didn't ask many questions. Life as he knew it came to a complete stop.

He remembered the conversation he had with Jenny on their first date. "There's a stream inside you," Jenny had said. "Not very many people see it. But it's there." Clipper believed those words that night. He replayed that moment in his memory over and over again. The words haunted him. They nestled deep inside his soul. He believed her. But during the past week, the stream had gone dry. Life was far less than meaningful.

In the Sanders' kitchen, Autumn and Felix were going through a reading comprehension drill. Felix had to read a five-paragraph story and then answer six questions. Autumn's eyes darted back and forth from Felix's worksheet to the stop watch. She drummed her fingers on the kitchen table, wondering when he would be able to finish reading.

"Time's up, Felix." Autumn said in exasperation. "We've got to get you to the point where you can read fast enough to have some time left over to answer the questions."

"I'm sorry, Miss Autumn."

"Don't be sorry, Felix. I'm not mad. It's just frustrating. How much did you finish reading when I called time?"

Felix scratched his head and spoke. "I was jes 'bout to the last coupla words."

"Well, then you're really close."

"I got tripped up on dat word there," the forty-three-year-old Cajun custodian said pointing at the word *hostility*.

"How long did it take you to get past it?"

"Bout a minute. I jes kept running it through my mind, and I couldn't sound it out," Felix replied.

"About a minute? Felix, if you see a word you're not sure about, don't let it trip you up! You could have answered all the questions in the amount of time it took you to work on that one word."

"I'm sorry, Miss Autumn."

"I told you that you didn't need to apologize. We're on the same team, and I'm your coach and—"

"I know dat."

"I'm encouraged though, Felix. I'm encouraged that if you use your time more wisely, you'll be able to pass this test. Let's just go over the review questions from the story," Autumn said as she picked up to read from the practice test. "What conflict greatly affected the Carter presidency?"

"Dat would be the Iranian hostility crisis."

"That's hostage crisis. But you would have recognized the answer in multiple choice."

"Ah sho would."

Autumn asked the next one. "Who was the president that followed Jimmy Carter?"

"Ronald Reagan."

"Right!" Autumn exclaimed.

Autumn's mom walked in the kitchen. "Autumn, you've got to be at volleyball in twenty minutes."

"Yikes! Well, Felix, you're going to do it."

"I sure do 'preciate it, Miss Autumn. I hope I don't let you down, now," Felix said as he picked up his book and headed to the door.

"You won't let me down. It isn't about me. This is for you."

"I know. I know. You done said that before," Felix said as

he opened the Sanders front door. "I'll see you at the school tomorrow."

Autumn's mom stared at her as Felix shut the door.

Autumn felt self-conscious. "What's the deal?"

"Nothing," Mrs. Sanders said.

"I know that look. What are you thinking?"

"I'm hesitant to say it because I know how much you really do care about him, but sometimes I wonder if you really *are* doing this for him."

"I *am* doing it for him." Autumn said defensively.

"Then don't be so wound up with him."

"Mom, I don't think I was that wound up," Autumn said, and then after a moment surrendered. "OK. Maybe I am pushing him hard, but I only have a few more days and then all I can do is watch—"

"And pray," Mrs. Sanders said with a smile.

Kandi returned from the student conference late Monday night. During the conference, she experienced several revelations about herself. She realized she had done a disservice to Clipper by not confronting him about all that she'd heard about him and Jenny. In the past, she tended to run from a potential problem rather than attack it head-on. Perhaps it was a habit she developed in an unstable home filled with physical threats from an alcoholic father and an emotionally weak mother. Whatever the case, she promised herself and God that she would speak the truth and not run away from difficult, even scary, things. She read the commitments she had made and had written in the back page of her Bible. She picked up the phone and dialed Clipper's number.

Clipper answered, "Hello?"

"Clipper?"

"Kandi?" Clipper said with surprise.

Kandi paced the floor with her heart racing. "How are you doing? We haven't talked in a long time."

Clipper felt the instinctive urge to give her a surface answer; instead he hesitated and spoke truthfully. "Things aren't good." When she didn't respond, Clipper tried to change the subject. "How was the conference?"

"We missed you," Kandi said.

"So is this some kind of outreach strategy that you learned?" Clipper asked cynically.

"Clip, please don't."

"OK."

"Justin told me that you heard what some people are saying," Kandi said.

"Yeah. He told me," Clipper replied.

"I wanted to call you earlier, but I thought that you wouldn't want to talk about it."

"I didn't a few days ago but . . ."

"I don't know what to say. Are you mad at me?"

"No." Clipper said quickly.

"That's a relief. Clipper, I really care about you, and I care about what's going on right now," Kandi said.

"If you really do care, why didn't you come talk to me about what people were saying?"

Kandi thought for a moment, weighing her words carefully. "I just wasn't sure how you'd react. I didn't want you to feel like I believed what—I was scared, Clipper."

"You *do* know I didn't sleep with Jenny, don't you?" Clipper asked.

"It wasn't that I didn't trust you. I just didn't trust Jenny."

Kandi knew she had said the wrong thing. Her hesitation and attempt to skirt around the question left her looking like she thought he had broken his vow of virginity. Her words and thoughts became jumbled. She didn't know what to say.

"I don't need this," Clipper said softly, angrily. "Why is it that Jenny is suddenly the enemy here?"

"I'm not the person you need to talk to, Clipper," Kandi said. "You need to talk to Melissa."

"Melissa?" Clipper said. "If she's involved, I am royally sunk. You actually listened to what she had to say?"

"We defended you and—"

Clipper jumped in. "*We* defended you? What's this *we* stuff? You and Justin listened to all this stuff and—"

"No, Autumn and I—"

"Autumn. I see. Should've known," Clipper said.

"We *did* defend you and we still—"

Clipper hung up the phone. Kandi ran her hands through her hair in frustration. She felt like a total failure. She had called to encourage him; instead, she gave him more reasons to explode.

Clipper grabbed the phone again and dialed a number. The line was busy so he reached for the car keys. He knew he could wait an eternity, and she still might be on the phone. His mom said with surprise, "I'm glad to see that you're getting out of the house. Is everything OK?"

"No, but that's life. I'll be right back," Clipper said without looking at her.

Clipper got in the car and took off down the road. The more he thought about it, the more he knew Melissa was at the bottom of all the lies. When did she become the "Talk Soup" hostess, reporting on the private lives of Summit High students for the general public? He always pitied her because she really had no life outside the realm of soaps, school gossip, and the telephone.

Clipper's anger intensified. He had thought about writing a note. But if he did, he knew she would take it, attach any meaning she wanted to it, and misquote it, and then she'd accuse him of harassing every woman he had ever had a conversation with. Her ways were absurd yet highly flammable. So he decided instead to confront her face-to-face.

He pulled up to Melissa's house and knocked loudly on the door. After a few moments, Melissa opened the door with a phone to her ear. She lifted a finger up to Clipper as a wait-a-second gesture.

"Uh-huh," she said, "I know, I don't believe it either. That's just what Lisa said that Jeff said he was gonna do." Another long pause added tension to the moment. "Well that's not what I think really happened." Finally Melissa looked back at Clipper and covered the mouthpiece, "Can you give me a sec? Why didn't you call me?"

"I tried, but the line's been busy."

"Oops. I had a friend on call waiting already I guess," she said smiling and then closed the door on him.

Clipper fumed, "Does this girl *ever* come up for air?"

He contemplated knocking on the door again, but instead sat down in the porch rocker to take a moment to cool down.

Finally Melissa came to the door. "Howdy, Clipper," she said, smacking her gum. "This is a really . . . an unusual gesture on your part. Coming over here, I mean," she said and then blew a pink bubble.

"This isn't a social visit. I didn't come here to chat or to find out what Jeff or Lisa or . . . or Elvis Presley is up to," Clipper said almost shouting.

"Gee wiz! Mom's asleep. Would you please, like . . . chill."

"I am incapable of chilling at this point."

"What is your deal?" Melissa said angrily.

"You want to know what *my* deal is? *This* is my deal. You are going around telling people that Jenny Elton and I had some kind of sexual thing going on. Excuse me, but I'm not aware of that. I think I'd know it if I did."

Melissa laughed out loud, "You're so funny."

"I'm not trying to be, Melissa. Believe me."

"Come on in, Clipper. Just please don't scream or I'll be, like, grounded for a lifetime. Mom has this like . . . super-acute migraine. Do you want to know the truth?"

Clipper stepped inside, and Melissa closed the door behind him. "I know the truth, Melissa. But apparently my friends have another opinion, and they all trace their knowledge back to you."

"If you would clam up for a second, I'll tell you what I told them and then you can tell me what the heck is going on," Melissa said angrily.

"I'm listening."

Melissa took a breath and started. "I know for a fact—*a fact*—Clipper, that she has been sleeping with someone. And you are the only guy that I know lately that she's been dating. Don't tell anyone this or I'm, like, . . . burnt toast. I read in her journal by accident, now listen close, *by accident,* the journal just sorta flipped open to a page where she happened to be writing. . . ." Melissa said, lying.

"And I guess you're going to tell me what this very private journal said. I can't believe you," Clipper said.

"It is important I think for you to know what kind of girl you've been dating. She's pregnant."

"That is a lie! It just isn't true."

"That's what I read."

"You read that I—?"

"It didn't say who got her pregnant. It just said that the tests came up positive, and she was pregnant and she was frightened about telling her parents and telling you. I just read a few sentences. I'm not making this up, Clipper! On top of that, just before I read the journal, I saw her puking her guts out in the school bathroom during a yearbook meeting," she said assertively and then warned him again. "If you tell anyone what I told you, you will pay big time for it."

Clipper was totally stunned. "She wrote that she was . . ." Clipper couldn't even say it.

"Pregnant," Melissa filled in the blank and then said it louder, "pregnant!"

Melissa's mom yelled from her bedroom, "What's that, honey?"

Melissa rolled her eyes, "Nothing, Mother."

Clipper's mind was reeling. "That's impossible," he said.

Melissa grabbed his arm, "Clipper, if it isn't true, why did she write it in her journal? I mean, if you are, like, totally not having sex with her, maybe it isn't you. But I know what I read."

She paused for a moment, thinking.

"I mean, she hasn't dated anybody else. Look, I blew it. I'm sorry. I shouldn't have mentioned it to anyone. For that I am like totally sorry. I was a dweeb for opening my mouth at all about it," Melissa said as her chin trembled. "But you know that's . . . just . . . me. I talk a lot."

Clipper walked toward the door, opened it, and then hurried to the car.

Melissa followed him out. "Clipper?" she called out.

But he acted as though he didn't hear her. He slammed his car door and drove away. He thought about the last night he had seen Jenny. She had changed from a confident person into a very distraught and confused little girl. All of the change, the sudden end of the relationship, the way she left so abruptly— it all made sense to him now. Part of him wanted to take every memento that he had saved from his three dates with her: the ticket stubs, the photos, the E-mail messages they had shared, the rose she had given him on their second date that he had pressed in a book—he wanted to take it all and burn it. And yet still another part of him wanted to run to her and to protect her. He drove around town praying and thinking about what he should do next.

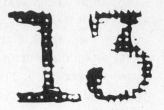

"Just don't get discouraged while you're in there. OK?" Autumn said as she drove Felix to Summit High for the GED exam.

"I'll do my best."

"I know you will," Autumn said, trying to mask her own nervousness. "Just remember to answer as many as you can, and don't get stuck on something you're not familiar with. And there will probably be some things on the test that we didn't cover. But don't let that trip you up. I know you can do it."

As they drove, Autumn tried to imagine what she'd say if he didn't pass the test. Felix could get so emotional about things. She prayed silently as she maneuvered through the Friday morning traffic.

"And remember, this is just the first part today. Tomorrow, you'll have the second part. You don't even have to worry about the reading comprehension segment. That's tomorrow," Autumn said.

"Autumn?" Felix said nervously. "I don't know if ole Felix can do dis test or not."

"You can't think that way, Felix. If you have that kind of mental attitude about this, you'll bomb. We've worked hard. You've worked hard. You deserve to pass it. You know this material. All your life you've had people tell you that you couldn't do it, and now I'm telling you that I believe you can."

"Maybe them other folks—"

"Those," Autumn said, correcting the pronoun, "Those other folks."

"Right. Maybe those other folks were dead right. Maybe I can't do this."

"Please!" Autumn said loudly. "I need you to believe that you can do this. We worked hard."

"Yeah, but you ain't—"

"Aren't, Felix aren't."

Felix continued, "You aren't goin' be in dere with me."

"Fine," Autumn said looking straight ahead at the road. "I am giving you the opportunity to really do something extraordinary, and you're throwing it away with that attitude. *Please,* would you give yourself a chance. Just this once, would you believe in yourself? I know you can do it, if you stop the negative thinking."

Autumn looked over at Felix. He was trembling as a tear rolled down his face. He quickly wiped it from his cheek. "I'll do it," he said in a broken voice.

Autumn realized what she had done. "Oh Felix. I'm sorry."

"No, Autumn. You're right. I need to quit talkin' like dat and thinkin' like dat."

As Autumn pulled into the parking lot, she questioned her motives. *Do I really want him to pass so that he can experience the thrill of personal accomplishment? Or is he just my little project? Some little medal to put on my uniform?*

As they got out of the car and walked toward the entrance, ten students ran out of the entrance and started chanting his name. "Felix, Felix, Felix . . ." They applauded as the stunned Felix LaBlanc walked toward them. Autumn, who accompanied Felix to the door, felt the surprise of the moment as well. After the applause died down, Felix thanked the students. He looked around for Clipper, whose absence seemed strange. Justin said to Felix, "Go in there and knock 'em dead Felix."

"Remember," another student said, "no matter what, you worked hard and gave it your best shot."

The other GED candidates walked by looking strangely at the cheering group at the entrance. The students gathered around Felix and prayed for him, then Felix slowly walked to the door and waved good-bye.

Autumn went over to Justin and Kandi. "Thanks, I know that meant a lot to him."

"Our pleasure," Kandi said. "Do you think he'll be able to do it?"

"Don't know," Autumn said. "I don't know how he'll do. It's hard for me to imagine him sitting in there for four hours. He is just so . . . active. His attention span is really slow. I'm wondering if this whole thing wasn't a big mistake."

"We just need to be prepared to break his fall if he fails."

"So it's today and tomorrow?" Justin asked.

"Right." Autumn said still looking away. "Where's Clipper?"

"We aren't sure where he is. I called him this morning, and he had already left the house," Justin replied. "We're planning on going out tonight to talk through all this junk."

Autumn asked, "Did he find out about the rumor?"

"Yeah, some guy came by and congratulated him on losing his virginity. It made him physically ill. What else could go wrong this month?"

Everyone left except Autumn. She stayed outside as if magnetized to the building. She brought a book to read, but her mind kept dancing back to Felix and the test.

Oh Lord, she prayed, *could you just settle his mind down? Keep him in there, Lord. Keep him on the task. He is so easily distracted. I don't know how to pray for Clip. But I know he needs you now perhaps more than he's ever needed you. I simply ask you to reassure him. Reassure him that you're there and that you're working all these things out. I don't know how involved Jenny and Clipper were physically, and I don't want to condemn him if he's made a mistake. Show me what to say and how to reach out to him. Hold him in your arms, Lord.* Her eyes moistened, *And Lord, hold me too.*

When Kandi got back home, she found a note that her mom left on the refrigerator door. It read:

Jenny called. She needs you to call her back ASAP.
Love you!
Mom

When she saw the note, her heart rate jumped. She dreaded hearing what Jenny might want her to know. She reached for the phone and dialed Jenny's number.

"Hello?" Jenny answered.

"Jenny, this is—"

"Hey Kandi. Thanks for calling me back so soon. Could I come over? We need to talk."

"Sure, Jenny. What do we need to talk about?"

"I . . . I can't say anything right now. I mean, over here. I'll have my mom drop me off if you can bring me back home."

"OK. Fine. I'll see you in a minute."

"Great."

Kandi wandered around the house like a zombie, looking out the window every thirty seconds as she waited for Jenny to arrive. "Why am I so stressed out about this? It is not my problem," she said aloud to herself. "But it involves Clipper. So it *is* my problem."

Jenny was at her door in less than ten minutes.

"Thanks for letting me come over."

"Sure, Jenny. How's Clipper?" Kandi asked, knowing fully Clipper's emotional state. She just wanted to appear oblivious, and she felt guilty for her deceptive question.

"Clipper and I stopped talking to each other," Jenny said awkwardly. "I mean, we just aren't hanging out together. Dating, I mean. Didn't you know that?"

Kandi now felt trapped in the lie, so she decided to come clean and everything came out at once. "Jenny, I'm sorry, I just wanted to know your side because Clipper has been a fairly unhappy camper these days, and we don't really talk that much. But I thought maybe you might have changed your mind about everything and maybe you've decided to have just a regular friendship with him or even might hang out together and maybe try to work things out because I know you really did have a good friendship. But after you date, that's kind of difficult to change—the relationship, I mean, into a friendship—"

Jenny interrupted her, "OK, I understand what your trying to say, Kandi. Could you just tell me what you know about the whole deal."

Kandi got louder. "I don't know anything, Jenny! I've *heard* lots, but I *know* little! And Clipper is *totally* in the dark too. How could you just leave him hanging like that, Jenny?"

"I don't need this. I do not need your condemnation. I'm dealing with enough of that without you piling on more. I know I handled this whole thing badly. That's why I came here. I need somebody to show me which side is up."

"I don't know if I can help you there," Kandi said in a cynical tone.

The two just stared at each other, both on the verge of tears. Kandi leaned against the kitchen counter in the classic defensive arms-crossed position. "You don't understand, Jenny. Clipper's like a brother to me. He's the brother I never had and I'm frightened. I'm scared half to death because he's hurting. You just walked out of his life without any explanation."

Jenny shook her head slowly then turn toward the door. Kandi walked over to her and said, "Jenny, I'm sorry. I want to help. I want to know what's going on."

"It's Tim."

"Tim?"

"I dated this guy for two years. He's at Notre Dame now. He's three years older than me. We broke it off around March of this year. Mom and Dad were thrilled because they knew that some things were just not right. Around Christmas last year he proposed to me."

"He what?"

"He proposed."

"As in marriage?" Kandi said more than a bit shocked.

"Yes, as in marriage. We really were in love. He even gave me a ring."

"What did you say?"

"I said yes, but I told him there would be no way my parents would take this. If they saw me with that ring on, they'd go nuts. A tenth grader and a college guy. They'd brand me with a scarlet A before they let us continue seeing each other after that. I just kept it in my purse and never showed it to anyone."

"So you said yes and kept it from your parents?"

"Right," Jenny said. "And after that, it was like we had no boundaries. We thought this was the real thing. We were going to be together forever, so the relationship kept getting more and more physical."

Kandi stood frozen in disbelief at Jenny's openness.

Jenny wept as she talked, wiping her eyes with her hand. "I never thought it would end. We were careful and took precautions, and there was very little guilt involved in all of this. We just knew we were going to be together."

"So he went off to college, and you decided to stay here and wait."

"I loved him so much. One weekend, I begged Mom to let me go up to Notre Dame with some friends for a basketball game. I had no interest in the game and they knew it. I just wanted to see Tim. Despite the fact that they had a perpetual frown on their faces the whole week before I went, they decided to let me go." Jenny said, almost smiling. "They knew the parents that would be going with us, so that made them feel better. Once we got there, I went to the place just off campus where Tim worked—a hole-in-the-wall pizza joint. I wanted to surprise him. I walked in and there he stood." She wiped her eyes again. "With a girl. She was all over him. I just walked over, grabbed his arm, put the ring he had given me on the bar, and ran away."

"What did he do?" Kandi asked.

"Nothing at all."

Jenny sat down on a stool in Kandi's kitchen. It was obvious to Kandi the story wasn't over and the worst was yet to come.

"For the next few weeks he called me, wrote to me, did anything he could to make it up to me, but I knew I couldn't trust him. Then one night he showed up at a party. He drove back down to Indianapolis just to be there because he knew I would be there. It was May 1st. I wish I would have never gone. I did the most insane thing I've ever done in my life. Since I planned on spending the night at Carla's house, I went there and got smashed."

"You got drunk at the party? Where were Carla's parents?"

"Carla's parents. Have you ever met them?"

Kandi shook her head.

"If you knew them, you'd understand," Jenny said as she stood up and looked out the window. "They practically organize these things. When Tim showed up, I was too wasted to even resist. After that night we E-mailed each other, called each other, and talked seriously about getting back together. How could I have been so stupid! Before that night, we'd been apart for almost two months. The relationship was completely over."

"So you decided to start over with the relationship?" Kandi asked.

"No. We decided that night was just a big mistake, and we wouldn't try to get the relationship going again. After a few weeks, I knew without a doubt I was pregnant."

The words she had dreaded hearing hit Kandi hard.

"And Tim acted like he had nothing to do with it. Finally, yesterday he tracked me down and handed me this."

Jenny pulled an envelope out of her purse and handed it to Kandi, who opened it nervously. The envelope contained a folded piece of paper, a business card and some hundred-dollar bills. Kandi read the note:

Jenny, I'm sorry things turned out the way they have, but I knew from the moment you said you were pregnant that you'd try to trap me into a long-term relationship. It just isn't what I want. And I don't think it is what you really want either. Think about it, Jenny. You're too young to have a child. And all that stuff about us getting back together. Don't flatter yourself. I have too many dreams to end up tied down to a wife and a kid. We both know what the right choice is. I'll be glad to pay for it. Inside this note is a card for a clinic. The three hundred dollars I'm enclosing should be more than enough money to cover the costs of solving the problem. I'm sorry things turned out the way they have, but you must come to the realization that it is over. I don't love you anymore.

Kandi folded the letter. Her hands trembled. She tried to speak in a tone that masked her emotions of shock, grief, and pity. "So what are you going to do?"

"Tomorrow, I'm going to get an abortion," Jenny said and started to cry. "Carla's taking me. I don't have a choice."

"Wait," Kandi said instinctively. "You *do* have a choice."

"No, I don't! What do you expect me to do? Do you think I should actually *have* this baby? Do you think I'd be able to survive the humiliation of being pregnant during my junior year at Summit? I'm not just doing this for myself. I'm doing it for Clipper. I'm doing it for my parents."

Kandi wasn't prepared for this kind of discussion. Strangely, she hadn't even thought that the conversation might lead down that road.

"What about the baby?" Kandi said.

"Please don't use that word," Jenny said.

"Why? That's not just a mass, a tissue growth. There are toes, fingers, and lungs forming inside you—a heart."

"Leave me alone!" Jenny screamed as she ran out of the house.

Kandi chased her, not knowing what to say. "Please, come back inside."

Jenny stopped and bent over, crying.

"I didn't mean to hurt you—"

"It's just that I've said what you are saying to myself a thousand times. I have dreams, nightmares of the clinic and the procedure. I don't want to do this. I hate myself for it."

Kandi jumped in, "You aren't doing it for you, Jenny. You're doing it to spare people pain. You are doing it for

Clipper's reputation, your reputation, your parents' reputation, but no, not for yourself. I know Clipper, he's the last person in the world that would want you to go through this for him."

"I can't talk about this with you anymore. Would you do something for me? Clipper called me and wanted to ask me about all of this. He's heard things. He needs to know the truth, and I can't lie anymore. Would you explain this to him?"

"But Jenny—"

"Please, Kandi? I can't face him. Would you please?"

Kandi whispered hesitantly, "OK, Jenny. OK."

Carla and Jenny agreed to meet at the jogging trail that day to discuss their plans.

"So you told him?" Carla said as she walked with Jenny in the park.

"Yes. I told him it was over. It was terrible. I felt like I was lying the whole time I was there." Jenny replied.

"You weren't lying, Jenny. You just didn't tell him the whole story. Let's face it. Clipper's a losing proposition from the word go. You need to start taking better care of your reputation. Summit High has clearly defined lines."

"Lines?" Jenny asked sincerely confused.

"Lines. Boundaries and groups. Clipper's in a certain group and you are in another. They just happen to be about as far from each other as you could possibly get. You've got a great future, Jenny. Your problem is you are way too sentimental and idealistic. I used to be just like you. I used to—"

"Save your breath Carla. It's over," Jenny said.

"Good. You don't need to be burdened down with him anyway."

Jenny looked away and said, "Can we just drop the subject?"

Carla handed Jenny a folded sheet of paper. "Here's the information. You're all set. Tell your mom and dad we're going shopping downtown and that you'll spend the night over at my place. That should give you some time to recover. And try not to think about it. Try as best as you can to put it out of your mind. So, tomorrow I'll meet you around nine, all right?"

"I don't know." Jenny said. "It's so fast. I don't know if I'm ready for this."

"Look, the longer you wait, the harder it will be to put this whole thing out of your mind. I don't see that you really have a choice in this. You've got to come with me—tomorrow. I've already set up the appointment."

"When I think about it, I feel like it'll take something important from me. Something—I don't know—sacred." Jenny said quietly.

"How can something so inconvenient be sacred or important?" Carla asked angrily. "If you don't do this, think about the hurt you'll cause your parents. Just tell them the truth, and you'll see how much they really love you. They'll throw you out on your ear, Jenny. I know you, Jenny. You want to live in a just world. But the world isn't right. You want love. But Tim is just an example of the fact that guys are jerks and love is for fairy tales and princesses. This isn't a fairy tale and you're not a princess. You are Jenny Elton. You are pregnant, and tomorrow you'll go with me to fix that mistake."

Autumn put down her novel and stood up quickly when she saw Felix heading out the door of the classroom.

"Well, my, my, Autumn, you been stayin' here da whole time? Shoooowee!"

"So how'd it go?" Autumn asked, trying to sound casual while dying to know.

"You know, Autumn, You a good teacher. I knowed a whole lot more now that I knowed when we started. But I don't know if I knowed enough. Just wish I was a better learner," Felix said while scratching his head.

Autumn squinted her eyes a bit, "That bad?"

"Jus don't want you to get your hopes up 'bout ole Felix, now. You done good."

"*Did* good, Felix. *Did* good." Autumn said, still preparing him for the writing he'd have to do on the next day's test.

Justin, overjoyed by Clipper's smile, jumped into Clipper's car that night. He feared the worst. Clipper had not been himself for days. But now, on the night that Justin expected to spend his time commiserating with Clipper about Jenny, he was greeted with a wide smile and a fresh new attitude.

"What're you up to?" Justin asked.

"Who, me?"

"Yes, you."

Clipper rolled down the window, letting in the warm night

air. "Free at last, free at last," Clipper said as his smile faded.

It spooked Justin. Clipper looked weird.

"I tell you," Clipper said after a moment, "I am so sick of girls."

"This wouldn't have anything to do with . . . Jenny, would it?" Justin said, lightly searching for a handle on the conversation. Clipper didn't answer. They just drove and listened to music. Justin tried to jump start the conversation. "So . . . like I said, this is your birthday so it's your choice. Where do you want to eat?"

"Not hungry," Clipper said tersely.

"So where are we going?"

"How about Riverdale?" Clipper said referring to a local bar.

"Riverdale?"

"Riverdale. Don't tell me you forgot about Riverdale. I remember you saying that you had a friend who let you in without being carded."

"Well yeah, but that was back when I was insane enough to think that was fun."

"Must be nice to have lived two lives," Clipper said.

"OK, is this some kind of joke?" Justin asked sincerely.

Clipper ignored the comment and opened the glove compartment and, to Justin's stunned shock and dismay, pulled out a pack of cigarettes. "Want one?" Clipper said to Justin. Justin swallowed and tried to digest the implications of what he was seeing.

"Come on. This was your brand. I remember seeing you light one up when you were a freshmen," he said coolly. "How do you open this stuff anyway?"

"OK. Fun's over," Justin said as he snatched the pack out of Clipper's hands and tossed the cigarettes out the window.

"Hey! That cost a heck of a lot of money," Clipper said angrily.

"Why don't you settle down?" Justin asked, raising his voice slightly.

"Me?" Clipper said loudly, "Settle down? I've been settled down all my life. I am the epitome of 'settled down.'"

Justin could only imagine where this night was headed. He shook his head and watched the oncoming traffic. He hated the idea of not being behind the wheel at that moment. He felt like he had been hijacked.

"Pull over, Clipper."

"What? Why?"

"Just pull over," Justin repeated.

"As you wish."

Clipper wheeled the car over to the shoulder of the old farm road. The wind brought the scent of rain to the area as a storm danced across the dark horizon. They parked a few yards away from an old rusted out bridge.

"What's with you?" Justin said angrily. "Are you making fun of me?"

Clipper didn't respond. He just walked around to the trunk of the car, opened it, and pulled out a six pack of beer.

Justin's eyes widened. "Oh, come on. Give me a break!"

Clipper sang loudly, "It's my birthday and I'll drink if I want to, drink if I want to, drink if I want to."

"I do *not* see the humor in this, Clipper." Justin said evenly.

"See, that's just it, Justin. Don't you get it?" Clipper said, then shouted, "You are looking at God's big joke. Clipper Hayes! Even his name is funny! Look at Clipper. He's only dated girls on formal occasions. Look at him try to be popular! Look at him try to fit in with more than three, yes, three people. Look at him fall in love! Look at him believe in her. Watch him! He thinks she really cares!"

A bolt of lightning miles away shot a flash of light followed by a rumble of thunder. "That's right, God. You did it! The joke's on me, ain't it?"

"Clipper. You are hacking me off. Big time."

"Good. Because see, I don't care. Me, I should be lucky that you're my friend. You, Justin, have a life! Yes, Grade A, verified, LIFE!"

"Quit it!"

"But me?" Clipper said as he jerked a can of beer off the plastic pack holder. "I'm the—"

"Drop the can!"

Clipper threw the open can at Justin and charged him as his anger finally exploded. He swung wildly at Justin, sometimes hitting him, but mostly missing. Justin didn't fight back. He simply dodged the punches and tried to hold his friend down. As Clipper fought he screamed, "I'm the joke! Can't you see that? Stay away from me!"

After Clipper lost the energy to punch, Justin plowed into his waist and drove him to the ground, yelling at his friend, "You can punch at me all night. But stop babbling on about being nothing! Don't you ever, *ever* say that to me again."

Suddenly Clipper's anger was gone, and he was weeping. He cried like a child. All the emotions that he locked deep down into his heart were released as he moaned, "She didn't even care about me," he said between gasps of air. "She didn't tell me what was going on. She told me it was over between her and Tim. She lied, Justin. She lied and I believed her."

"Hey," Justin said, trying to stop the outburst of tears and anger, "Hey, now, I know. It's tough, but she didn't mean to hurt you. She wanted to spare you all the gory details. She didn't want to disappoint you."

"She couldn't. I loved her too much," Clipper said still trying to catch his breath. "I would have done anything for her."

"I know, Clipper. I know."

They talked for over an hour that night as they watched the thunderstorm crawl closer to them. But before they knew it, the wind subsided and the clouds evaporated, leaving them dry under a starry sky. They dumped the beer into a dumpster and headed home.

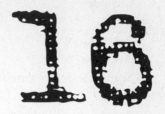

16

At 7:30 the next morning Autumn found herself at Summit High School alone for the second straight day of reading, worrying, praying, and waiting as Felix took the final segments of his high school equivalency exam. She was already beginning to prepare for the worst. She'd tell him once again that the important thing was that he gave his all to the challenge. She'd remind him of all he had learned through the process.

Still, she didn't lose all hope. She imagined what it would be like if they received word he had passed. What a moment of victory that would be!

Clipper awoke to a soft knock at his bedroom door and the tentative voice of his mom. "Clipper? Are you awake?"

The morning sun blinded him as he covered his face with a pillow.

"Clipper?"

"Yes?"

"Are you awake?"

"Am now, Mom."

"Someone left a letter under our front door last night," his Mom said.

Clipper stumbled over to the door, opened it, and took the letter. "Thanks," he said groggily. He closed the door and stared at the letter. After a moment, he opened it and read:

Dear Clipper,

I'm writing you to let you know something that I should have told you the night I came over to tell you that I didn't want to see you anymore. People have talked to you and have even blamed you for being a part of my situation. Somehow people found out about it, and the next thing I knew, both your friends and mine had come to the conclusion that my present state had to do with our relationship. I'm so sorry. I thought about calling you many times, and I really wanted to have your support, but I knew how much the news would hurt you. I had this fantasy that I could keep it all to myself, but it just didn't turn out that way. This will all change today. I am going with a friend to correct the problem.

Clipper stopped reading and looked away trying to understand what she meant by "correct the problem." He went back to the letter for more clues.

I want you to know that I admire you. You are a gentleman. I also want you to know that I meant every word that I said to you. The stream is real in your life. And I know where it comes from. It took me awhile to come to this conclusion because I had lots of doubts about God. But the stream has something to do with your belief in God.

There are very few guys out there like you. Be proud of your standards. I would be. I wish there was a way I could go back and relive the past year, but I can't. There's no way for me to ever be what I used to be. The scars will always be a part of my life. Even after I marry, they'll be there. When my children grow up, they'll still be there. I threw it all away because I thought I could break the rules for the sake of true love. I've learned now that true love obeys the boundaries. It isn't selfish. It stands up for what is right. And that's what you do constantly.

After last night, Clipper thought, *I'm not sure I'm exactly who she thinks I am.* Then he read the last few sentences of the note.

I hope you'll forgive me for not being up front about everything. I don't expect you to feel the same way about me that you did before all of this came down, but I hope we'll still be friends.
                                        Love,
                                        Jenny

He stood in his bedroom staring at the letter, totally perplexed by what Jenny had written. His eyes scanned up the letter to the sentence—*This will all change today. I am going with a friend to correct the problem.*

Then he felt a desperate sense of urgency. He took the letter and stuck it in his sock drawer. He jumped into the shower, and dressed.

As he headed for the back door, his dad stopped him.

"Whoa! Time out!" Clipper's dad said, while slurping on an oversized cup of coffee. "Where's the fire?"

"Hey, Dad."

"How was the night on the town with Justin?"

"Weird," Clipper said.

"Weird?" His dad said with a perplexing look on his face.

"I'll explain later, Dad."

"So no milk? No Pop Tart? No cereal? It's the most important meal of the day!" his dad said, sounding like a commercial. "I'd like to talk to you for a few minutes."

"Dad, this is really not a good time at all." Clipper said.

"Is someone's life in danger?" Dad said with a laugh.

"Yes. As a matter of fact."

His dad frowned, more than a bit concerned.

Clipper tried to explain quickly so he could scram. "Not my life. It's just that someone's about to make a decision, and I need to be there."

"I don't know what in the world you're talking about."

"Just trust me. Please, Dad."

After a short moment his dad surrendered with a sigh.

As Clipper drove down the boulevard that led to Jenny's neighborhood, he prayed, "God, I don't know why I'm doing this. Is it instinct, or you, or my own selfishness or my stupidity?

But I need you to guide me. I've been a bit wacko. OK, very wacko in the past twenty-four hours. I'm sorry, God. I've trusted you, and you've taken care of stuff in the past. Why should I believe that you'd turn your back on me right now? I don't want to hide the truth about your forgiveness. I don't want that message to remain locked inside of me. I want your truth to run wild."

He turned into the subdivision whispering, "Be there, Jenny. Be there." As he approached the house, he saw Carla's Neon backing out of Jenny's driveway. The car headed toward him on the drive exiting the subdivision. He tried to get their attention, but they didn't even see him. He quickly made a U-turn to follow her car. "I can't believe I'm doing this," he said to himself.

He looked down at his fuel gauge and panicked. His car only had about an eighth of a tank of gas, and he had absolutely no idea where he was going. The Neon switched lanes erratically as they approached the interstate on ramp. "Oh great," he said angrily to himself, knowing that they could be heading out of state for all he knew. He punched the steering wheel with his palm in frustration. He stayed a few car lengths back, but kept them in clear view. Clipper's heart pounded as he glanced at the fuel gauge every few seconds. He wondered if this same God that broke five loaves to feed a multitude could spontaneously inject his car with gas. He doubted he had the faith to provoke that kind of miraculous intervention.

As they approached downtown, he followed as the girls switched lanes to exit. *Finally,* Clipper thought. They turned onto a busy street filled with the tourists and families that

show up in droves on Saturday mornings in the downtown
area. After a mile or so of very slow moving traffic, he felt his
car sputter and cough. The dreaded had occurred. He pulled
the slowing car over to the side of the street. He was grateful
for the free weekend parking, otherwise this excursion would
have cost an extra thirty dollars in parking tickets from the
ever-present meter patrol. He jumped out and hurried to see
if he could keep up with the car on foot. Traffic lights and
bumper-to-bumper congestion became his allies, but he still
had no time to waste. The cars stopped at a light three blocks
into the foot race, and Clipper saw his chance. With pains
shooting through his oxygen-starved lungs, he sprinted
toward the Neon. He was only a few feet away when the light
turned green.

"Jenny!" Clipper screamed out while waving his hands,
even though he knew she probably couldn't hear or see him.
A taxi pulled beside Clipper as he dropped to one knee in total
exhaustion. He prayed aloud between gasps, "Lord—I
thought—it was you that wanted this—but musta been me—
What now?"

"Hey kid," the weathered-looking Hispanic taxi driver said
loudly, as he pulled over to the side of the street. "It's a whole
lot easier in a car," the man said with a laugh. "Hop in."

Clipper opened the back door and jumped in. "Follow that
Neon," he said dramatically.

"Your wish is my command," the taxi driver said with a
smile. He jerked the car back on to the road, switched lanes,
and maneuvered around the traffic like a pro. Clipper wondered if the guy had done this in movies.

"Whoa!" Clipper said as he was tossed from side to side in the speeding vehicle.

"Seat belts. Seat belts," the taxi driver said, keeping his eyes on the road.

"I only have two dollars."

"I don't care, kid. Consider this gratus," He said, smiling at Clipper in the rear view mirror. "Girl trouble?"

Clipper paused, wondering if he should get into the whole sordid story with a stranger. He decided simple and vague was the best. "Actually, well, she is a girl and—"

"Jenny?" the cab driver asked.

"Yes, Jenny. How did you—"

"Well, kid, everybody downtown knows her name, the way you were screaming it out. You must love this Jenny girl, huh?" he said as he finally caught up with Carla's Neon. Clipper didn't respond so the driver clarified. "Not just anyone would go to this kind of trouble for someone, unless they really love them."

"It's not like that," Clipper tried to explain. "It's not your basic romance. Believe me, not at all basic. I mean, I do love her, but it's not like—"

"Not talkin' 'bout no lovey-dovey love? You talkin' 'bout the real deal?" the driver interrupted.

Clipper spoke in fragments, his mind still on Carla's Neon. "I don't know if I can . . . it's like . . . I mean, it's a God kind of love, I guess you could say."

Clipper couldn't believe what he was saying, to a cab driver, of all things.

"Hey, that's the best kind of love, the right kind," the driver answered, with a smile.

Now Clipper couldn't believe what he was hearing. He just nodded his head once again.

"Girl's lucky, I tell ya. It's a rare thing to have someone who would run through the streets of Indianapolis for 'em. I'm telling you she is a very, very lucky girl. Lucky, lucky, lucky."

There was silence in the car for a moment. Clipper didn't feel like he could bring anybody luck. Finally, the man spoke again, "Nah, not lucky. That's not the word I'm thinkin' 'bout. I guess the word's blessed. Yeah. That's it. She's blessed."

"I just have to talk to her before she—"

The driver interrupted again. "God gonna use you?"

"I hope so. You know I asked God for a sign, and he . . . he gave me a cab ride," Clipper said, overcome with emotion mixed with relief.

"I knew it! I knew somethin' was different about you, kid," the driver said, smiling into the rearview mirror.

"I've got to stop her. I'm afraid she's going to do something she might regret, and I've got to talk to her."

"Then go for it, my boy. Yell, plead, let her know what you're thinking. It might not look right to the normal outsider, but they don't matter. You have to go with your heart. Even if it makes you look like a fool. Ooooooh, me! I love a good chase in the middle of the day!"

"She's slowing down," Clipper said.

The driver looked in sudden disbelief as they passed a large group of demonstrators waving picket signs and chanting slogans. The Neon parked in a small lot next to a small medical center. He read the sign, "Indiana Family Planning Corporation."

"You know what place this is, don't you, kid?" the driver said.

"An abortion clinic."

"That's right. You sure about this?"

They watched Carla and Jenny walk quickly past the screaming, banner-waving crowd of activists.

Clipper's heart raced as he spotted a news crew outside. He swallowed and then said softly, "It's not my baby."

"Doesn't matter though, does it?" the taxi driver said.

"No," Clipper said as he pulled the two dollars out of his pocket.

The taxi driver waved it off. "I told you. It's on me."

"Thanks. I can't tell you how much I appreciate it," Clipper said.

"Don't mention it. Just get on in there. You've got somebody counting on you," he said.

Clipper reached over to him to shake his hand, "Thanks, uh . . ." He said looking for the driver's name on his ID, which hung from the rearview mirror. "Thanks . . . Roberto?"

"Roberto. Roberto Hernandez."

"Thanks, Roberto," Clipper said in a daze as he stumbled out of the car onto the pavement.

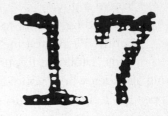

When Clipper walked into the large waiting room, he saw Jenny sitting next to Carla filling out a form. Carla glanced up and saw Clipper standing in the entrance. Carla's face communicated her shock . . . and displeasure. Carla whispered something to Jenny, who continued to write without looking up. Carla got up and walked over to Clipper, grabbed him by the arm, and pulled him into a hallway out of Jenny's sight.

"What do you think you're doing here?" Carla whispered angrily.

"I'm here to support Jenny in a difficult situation," Clipper replied.

"What does *this* have to do with *you?*"

"What does this have to do with *you?*" Clipper countered angrily.

"I'm her friend, Clipper," Carla said emphatically.

"So am I."

"You're a guy."

"No kidding. I want to talk to her."

"Funny. Please tell me that this is some kind of joke."

"Carla, I followed your car all the way into town, not having any idea where you were going, I ran out of gas on the way because I didn't want to lose the two of you. By the way, everyone in Indianapolis would appreciate you using a turn signal every now and then!"

"Very funny, Clipper."

"And then I chase your car for about a mile downtown. I get in a cab, and . . . you think this is a joke? You barely know me and I barely know you. Different species in the social strata, but believe me when I say that this is no joke. I am *not* kidding. I'm *going* to speak to her."

"This is highly inappropriate," Carla said.

"And who are you? Her mom?"

"I'm a friend, looking out for her best interest. What's best for *her* . . ." Carla finished as she crossed her arms.

"And so am I," Clipper said, crossing his arms.

They stood there staring at each other. Then Clipper broke the silence. "Look, why don't you go over there and tell her that I'm here. Tell her that I just want to talk to her, and if she doesn't want to see me, I'll leave."

"Fine," Carla said.

Clipper regretted the proposal the moment he laid it out. Jenny could simply shake her head and all the driving, screaming, chasing, bumming, and pleading would be for naught.

Clipper peeked around the corner as Carla walked over to Jenny. She leaned down and said something. Jenny looked over at Clipper, who waved slightly. Jenny looked embarrassed at first. She listened intently as Carla continued talking. When Carla stopped, Jenny looked at Clipper, then back at Carla and nodded. Carla was whispering loudly and gesturing with both hands, obviously upset.

Clipper kept praying as he watched.

Finally Carla grabbed her purse, stood, and walked over to Clipper and said, "She's all yours."

"You're leaving?"

"Yes."

"But my car ran out of gas about—"

"You figure it out, Clipper. You found a way to get here. You can find a way to get back. I know what's best for her even though both of you seem to be confused. She hasn't decided what she's going to do, but I'm not going to get into some . . . some morality debate. I'm going. Just remember, Clipper, it's her choice."

As Carla opened the door, the sounds of protest chants and traffic filled the sterile waiting room. Clipper walked up to Jenny. She stood and embraced Clipper, crying now, "I'm sorry, Clipper. I'm so sorry. I'm scared. My back's against the wall, and I don't know what to do."

Clipper didn't know what to say. He didn't have any easy answers, but he did know what the right answer was. "Let's go back home."

"I don't think I can."

"You can, Jenny. Let's just go back. I know this is none of my business. You make the choice. But talk to Autumn. She can help you."

"Why are you doing this?" Jenny asked suddenly. "Think about your own reputation. People will know that I'm pregnant and they'll suspect you are the father."

"I know the truth," Clipper said sincerely, "and so do you."

"I just feel like my life is over."

"It's not over. Think about the baby."

"I can't."

"But you have to. You know, I was the last child in our family. My sister and brothers are at least twelve years older than me. I was definitely unplanned. My parents always said that my birth brought them a second chance in life." Clipper looked deep into her eyes, wishing he could reach into her troubled soul.

"How's that?" she finally asked.

"You can probably guess that they didn't want another child. The pregnancy really turned my dad against my mom. They almost divorced. A day before they scheduled a quiet, very private abortion, a friend came by. Dad said she didn't have any idea what was going on, but she talked to them for hours. She told them God had a plan for their lives and that he knew them before they were even born. That really had an impact on them at the time. Mom said it helped her realize that if God knew her before she was born then God knew me—the baby inside her. She had never thought of it that way. The friend had an impact on Dad too. They changed their minds and, lucky for me, didn't get the abortion."

Jenny looked up at Clipper as he said "Will you just come with me? You've got lots of friends, and I know your parents will be upset, but they love you, Jenny."

Jenny stood and curled into Clipper's embrace. As she softly cried, she said, "I'm so scared, Clipper."

"I am too," he replied softly. "But if you do this, if you stay here and go through with it, you can't un-abort a baby."

Clipper searched for the right words, and when he opened his mouth again, he truly did not know what would come out. "Jenny, you are a believer in streams. I remember you telling me that you believed in streams underneath the surface. And you said that some people are lava. You go deep under the surface, and you'll get burned. That's not you, though. You can see that stream in me because you have one yourself."

"Oh God, if only I did," she cried.

"You do, Jenny. You do. You can hold onto it and face anything with courage. It's a gift from God. He doesn't want you to give it away."

"How can I even call out to him? I feel so ashamed," Jenny whispered.

"I'm not ashamed of you, Jenny. And I know God isn't either. The best time to talk to God is when you are ashamed. You made a mistake, but an abortion won't solve anything."

Jenny sat for a long time. She closed her eyes and sat motionless. Clipper's heart pounded. He couldn't think of anything else to say. The sudden silence accented the sounds around them: the phone ringing, the muffled sounds of angry protesters, the echoes of hard heels on the wooden floor, the sound of Jenny's breath, the slow drone of passing cars . . .

"Jenny Elton?" The receptionist called out in a loud voice that resonated in the room like Judgment Day. Jenny flinched. She shook her head and walked out of the clinic with Clipper.

"I don't know what to do now. My car's a few miles away," Clipper said.

Jenny gave him a strange look.

Clipper raised his eyebrows and said after a sigh, "It's a long story."

Clipper looked across the street and to his surprise he saw Roberto, the old taxi driver, leaning up against his yellow cab with a smile on his face. He waved them over for another free ride.

Autumn wrote in her journal the following Wednesday:

Life is full of waiting. I'm doing my share of waiting. My father says that one of the sure signs of becoming a fully devoted follower of Christ is patience. I have to confess that I'm not quite there yet. In about an hour, I'll find out if Felix passed the GED. And I'm about to go nuts. Clipper and Justin asked if they could come with us. The person I'd really like to be there for support is Kandi. But would she drop her schedule to join me on this highly stressful occasion? Nope. Yes, I'm mad. UGH! She had some kind of meeting to attend. She didn't go into very much detail. Another sign that the BurgeRama gang just ain't what it used to be.

Clipper sounds great, considering all he's been through lately. He has an incredible heart. Dad and I went over to Jenny's house yesterday to support her while she told her parents

*about the pregnancy. They were very hurt by it all, but we left
with great hope that reconciliation and support would be provided. Truth hurts, but it also heals.*

Autumn heard Justin's horn, closed her journal, and hurried
out to the car to greet Justin, Clipper, and Felix. "Morning,
guys."

"Don't know bout all ya'll goin' down with me," Felix said.
"I thinks I got little chance to pass dis."

"Well, Felix, you gave it your best, didn't you?" Justin said.

"I believe I did."

"Then no matter what happens, you should be proud."

As they negotiated through the morning traffic, Clipper and
Justin dominated the conversation discussing their upcoming
senior year, their budding careers at the BurgeRama, and the
rising prices of athletic shoes. When they finally came up for
air, they noticed that Autumn and Felix were unusually silent.

"Autumn," Clipper said, "You all right?"

"Peachy," she replied.

"Felix?" Justin said.

"I'm doin' OK."

Clipper said, "I know that you two are nervous about this,
but there's nothing you can do about it now. So let's just relax
and enjoy the moment."

"Is this the Clipper I know?" Autumn said. "The guy who
can't talk to a girl or play in a basketball game without reading
three or more self-help books?"

Clipper smiled, "Those days are over. You're looking at a
totally new me."

"Really?" Autumn replied. "Looks like the same guy to me. Brain transplant? New girlfriend? Publisher's Clearing House winner?"

"None of the above. I'm just not going to take life so seriously now. I've nixed my plans to be a monk," he said faking seriousness. "I've decided not to shave my head, live in a cave, and survive on a diet of oat bran, soy, and bean sprouts. I'm just gonna get on with my life."

"Whatchu talk'n 'bout there, Clipper?" Felix asked.

"He was just joking," Autumn explained.

Clipper continued, "I've decided that I have been putting way too much effort into trying to be a success. God knows who I am and what I need. I don't need to spend half my life worrying about what other people think, or who I'm going to date, and how I'm going to make a living. Just going to live life to the fullest and let God handle the big stuff."

"Sounds like a plan," Justin said.

"And I'm expecting all of you to do the same," Clipper continued. "Especially you, Felix. If you don't pass this thing, it isn't the end of the world. You don't need some piece of paper to tell you that you're somebody. You're God's man, Felix."

Justin nosed in, "So does this sudden philosophical speech mean you're going to be a preacher?"

"Nope. Just means this is a new day," Clipper replied.

They were quiet as they turned onto the boulevard heading toward Summit. Autumn finally spoke up tentatively, trying not to sound nosy to Clipper, "So, uh, how's Jenny doing?"

"She's doing great. We're still friends. Good friends. By the way, thanks for going over there and supporting her. She called me after you left."

"How did she sound?"

"She sounded pretty good. She knows that this is going to be tough on her whole family, but they're willing to support her. She said she has the option of moving out of town. She hasn't made up her mind yet."

He paused, then said, "You should have seen Mom and Dad's faces when I told them Jenny was pregnant."

"What did you say?" Autumn asked, leaning forward to hear his answer.

"I was pretty emotionally upset at the time. It was after I got back from the clinic. I just walked in and bawled like a baby. I didn't even think about how it looked. About five minutes into the thing, I noticed they had this glazed look on their faces. Like I had just died or like I was about to die. Suddenly I realized what they thought had happened. I just said, 'Whoa! Hold on a sec. I didn't do anything like that. It's not mine.'"

"Did they believe you?" Justin asked.

"They thought about it for a minute or so. I figure they put the pieces together—we'd only been out a few times and usually with friends. Think about it. Could they really believe that I'd do that? No way. I'd have to break lots of promises to myself, to God, and to them. It didn't take them long to get everything back into the right perspective, their vital signs returned, they started breathing normally, and everything was hunky-dory. They were very cool about it. But it did scare the bejeevers out of them."

Justin pulled into the parking lot. "Ready or not . . ." he said, "here we are."

Justin, Autumn, and Clipper got out of the car. It took a second before they realized that Felix wasn't moving. Justin opened the door for him. "Uh, Felix. We're here. So why don't you come along with us."

"Don' think I better."

"What?"

"Don' think I better go with you up there."

"Why not?" Justin asked pleadingly.

Autumn interrupted Justin, whispering to him, "Justin, let me. You guys go on ahead and let me talk to him."

Felix looked up at Autumn. She knew this whole event was disturbing to him. "Scoot over, Felix." Felix moved to the center of the back seat. Autumn got in next to him, leaving the door open to take advantage of the morning breeze.

"I don' think I should go. Don' think I passed dat there test, no."

Autumn sighed. "Felix, I've told you a hundred times that—"

"I know. I done ma best, but I caused you trouble if I flunked. I wasted your time."

"Felix. You didn't waste my time. I had a chance to teach, and you learned lots this summer. I want you to know that if you didn't even take the test, I'd still have done it. I found out I'll still get to jump to my junior year with the credits I have. Besides, look at what you've accomplished. You solved problems and written sentences with words you never knew before this summer. You know Walt Whitman and C. S. Lewis. You learned how to divide, and you learned about the founders of the Constitution. You learned some things that many people don't know. So don't think of this as some kind of waste. You did well. If you didn't pass, you're still Felix. You stood up for Kandi earlier this year with all that stolen computer business. That changed her future. You are a very faithful friend. That's something that you don't learn in books. It doesn't have anything to do with the head. It has to do with the heart. And you have one of the biggest hearts in Indianapolis."

Felix wiped his eyes. "OK," he said quietly, "I guess we should go."

Felix and Autumn caught up with Justin and Clipper who were waiting nearby.

"Sure are a lot of cars here," Autumn observed.

"It's a parent-faculty meeting," Justin said.

"Oh yeah. Dad told me he was going to be there," Autumn said.

They walked to the office. The hall was desolate as they walked toward the front office.

All four were a bit jumpy with expectation of the test results. The secretary took Felix's test results out of the file and handed it to him.

Justin, Clipper, and Autumn stood back to give Felix some room as he read the results. He opened the envelope and pulled out a thin, blue computer print out. They watched him as his eyes slowly scanned the paper.

He shook his head and surrendered the report to Autumn.

Autumn said calmly, "It's OK."

"But I didn't pass." Felix said stone-faced.

"But you did well. You came really close." Autumn said trying to hide her disappointment.

"I'm sorry," Felix said in a sorrowful tone.

"Felix, don't let this discourage you," Autumn said with assertiveness. "You came up a little short, but it is OK."

"But what about your class? You gonna miss out on those extra college hours." .

"It doesn't matter."

Justin cleared his throat and said, "Felix, I think those results are really insignificant. Come with me."

Felix held up his hands and said, "Justin, I think Ole Felix needs to just get back to work. You all can go back home. I'll find a ride back."

"Where are you two going?" Autumn said. "I need a ride home. I have some—"

"We need *both* of you to come in here," Clipper interrupted in a obviously hinting voice.

When Kandi poked her head into the hall from the auditorium, Autumn knew something strange was about to happen.

"So what's the meeting, Kandi?" Autumn asked. "I thought you said you couldn't be here."

"Just get in here!" Kandi demanded in an excited whisper.

The four walked to the auditorium, and as soon as they entered they were greeted by over two hundred people. Students, faculty from Summit, and lots of others stood and cheered. Ms. Jarvis threw a blue satin graduation robe over Felix's shoulders.

Autumn stood in total shock at what she was watching. She feared this was a big mistake. How could they make such a mammoth assumption that Felix would pass the GED? She tugged on Ms. Jarvis' sleeve and said loudly over the cheers of the crowd. "Ms. Jarvis! There's been a big mistake. He didn't pass the test. He did well but—"

"This isn't about the high school equivalency test. Just put this on and come up on stage," Jarvis said in Autumn's ear as she handed Autumn a robe. Still in shock, she donned the robe and zipped up the front over her clothes. Ms. Jarvis made insistent gestures for them to follow her.

Autumn's heart was in her throat. She had participated in a score of debate tournaments, but she had never been this nervous. Felix and Autumn followed Ms. Jarvis, the principal of Summit High, up the side stairs onto the platform of the auditorium. They walked awkwardly, not knowing what was going to happen.

As Felix's eyes scanned the crowd, he saw retired teachers and students who graduated years ago as well as parents, current students, and faculty members. Autumn and Felix both smiled politely. Autumn's mind raced, wondering what was happening.

"What we doin' up here?" Felix asked Autumn. "I didn't pass dat test."

Finally the applause died down. Autumn glanced as the man who stood next to them moved to the podium. He looked familiar to Autumn, but she still couldn't place him. Ms. Jarvis tapped the microphone and began.

"Thank you all for being here. We wanted this to be a surprise, and I think we succeeded." The crowd applauded once more. "I'd like to thank both our U.S. House Representative Edward Hatchfield and Dr. Harold Connell, the president of Indiana State University, for being here for this very special occasion. Dr. Connell?"

Dr. Connell walked to the podium. "We are here to honor a person who has been an outstanding citizen and a faithful servant of public education for over twenty years. As you know, each year Indiana State University honors the work of one person who has made a contribution to education and the well-being of the youth of our state. We receive nominations from almost every county in Indiana for this recognition. Usually we honor public school teachers, principals, or, on some rare occasions, parents. But this year, after receiving a wave of nominations, we are proud to honor Felix LeBlac with an honorary doctorate from Indiana State University for over twenty years of extraordinary service to students, teachers, and parents."

The audience stood to their feet and applauded as Felix whispered to Autumn who stood overwhelmed, "Autumn! Autumn, didn't they know I fail de test?"

"Felix, I don't think that really matters right now," She said with her eyes wide, "I think you're going to be a doctor!"

Congressman Hatchfield, who happened to be a former student from Summit High in the late seventies, read his commendation, "I'll always remember Felix for being a person who did everything he was asked to do and doing it without complaint. We rarely thanked him when I was here. But no one could ignore the time he spent on the job. He was always the first one to open up and was always here after the last person left. He loved the teachers and the students very deeply."

Then Hatchfield invited Kandi to speak. Kandi stood at the microphone and spoke, "I am grateful to Felix because more than once he sacrificed time and reputation to help me through really tough times. He showed me what it means to be a faithful friend. He's the kind of guy that, well, if you asked him to mop the moon, he'd find a way to do it. He's kind and compassionate. He doesn't envy, he doesn't boast. He is love with calloused hands. That's what he represents to me. And Felix and I have another thing in common. We have a great friend named Autumn, who never ceases to amaze me by always wanting the best for me and for all her friends. She's certainly had an big scholastic impact on Felix. I'm looking at Felix's scores. He missed passing his G.E.D. by only a few points. And he's a guy who was told he'd never make it to junior high. One of Autumn's favorite scriptures is in the Book of James, I think. It says, 'faith without works is dead.' And Autumn has a ton of both. I love you, Autumn!"

The crowd stood and applauded heartily. Representative Hatchfield gestured to the crowd to be seated while he read other letters of commendation. Finally, Rep. Hatchfield asked Felix to join him and Dr. Connell at the podium. "We want to encourage you to not give up on your dream of passing the G.E.D. We also want to encourage Autumn Sanders, your tutor, who has spent the better part of her summer helping you. We thank her for taking time to help you pursue something that others discouraged you to pursue. We know your future is bright."

"Hopefully, we'll see you at Indiana State," Dr. Connell interjected. Then in a more formal voice, Connell continued, "Felix. Because of your energy and your ability to succeed and be faithful with what you have been given, we present you with this Honorary Doctorate in Education and Social Work."

The crowd stood once again and applauded as Dr. Connell handed Felix the diploma and placed a medallion with a colorful ribbon around his neck. Felix's eyes scanned the crowd. Tears rolled down his cheeks when he spotted his elderly parents. Representative Hatchfield, Dr. Connelly, and Principal Jarvis encouraged Felix to say a few words, but he couldn't speak. He was overwhelmed by all he had experienced.

Kandi and Autumn embraced as Clipper and Justin lifted Felix onto their shoulders. The applause from the audience intensified as Felix sported a grin from ear to ear.

Thanks for visiting Summit High. I'd love to hear from you
if you ever want to ask a question, swap stories,
need prayer, or even vent about life in general.
My E-mail address is mtullos@lifeway.com
See ya!
Matt Tullos